LUKE DAWSON: WELLS FARGO GUN

LUKE DAWSON: WELLS FARGO GUN

•

Denny Andrews

AVALON BOOKS
NEW YORK

Published by Thomas Bouregy & Co., Inc.
160 Madison Avenue, New York, NY 10016

Library of Congress Cataloging-in-Publication Data

Andrews, Denny.
    Luke Dawson : Wells Fargo gun / Denny Andrews.
        p. cm.
    ISBN 978-0-8034-9841-9 (hardcover : acid-free paper)
    I. Title.

PS3601.N55263L85 2007
813'.6—dc22

                                        2007007975

PRINTED IN THE UNITED STATES OF AMERICA
ON ACID-FREE PAPER
BY HADDON CRAFTSMEN, BLOOMSBURG, PENNSYLVANIA

To Lorna—without her this couldn't have been written.

Chapter One

OUTSIDE LAWRENCE, KANSAS 1863

The sun shone warm that early June. A soft breeze kissed the gently flowing wheat. A horse clopped to the water trough. A cow bawled looking for its calf.

Merle Dawson screamed. It wasn't so much a scream of pain as it was shrill and angry. From his hiding place under some brush, Merle's five year old son Luke suppressed a giggle. His mom had played this game with him many times before. If he stayed silent and still, no matter what, he received a little piece of peppermint candy as a reward. If he came out of his hiding place, he got nothing. Sometimes he was scolded. Today he was going to get that candy for sure. He wouldn't budge until he heard, "Ally ally out, Lukey, ally ally out." If his mom yelled, "Come out, Lukey," or "All right Luke, come here," that didn't count. He had to stay where he was or no candy.

Merle had spotted the three riders before Luke saw them. She said calmly, "Luke, go hide." Luke saw the riders in the distance with their strange mixture of uniforms, North and South, and the straw slouch hats. Then he sprinted to his hiding place. It was a hole in the ground with a wooden roof and concealed by bushes. They had company coming and Luke hoped his mom would call him out soon.

Now Luke heard his mom scream again. She had yelled before and even screamed. It seemed somehow different to him this time. Then he heard the gunshot. Powder and lead cost money. His mom had never pulled that trick on him before.

Luke very carefully raised the lid of his hideout. He saw one of the men coming out of his house. In his hand he had a Humrino's Best flour sack with just a few items in it. The other two were looking down at the ground and talking. "Man, I sure didn't want to do that. Not yet, at least."

"It was a waste sure enough, Billy Fred. But if I hadn't done it, she was gonna separate your head from your body with that sickle there."

"Anybody else 'round?" asked the first man.

"Didn't see anybody," replied the second.

"Let's go," the third said.

With that, they mounted up and headed south at a

leisurely pace. Luke waited. He waited for another hour. His mom had never left him there this long. Finally, he came out from under his hiding place. It was quiet. Luke walked into the barnyard. His mom was lying down. A sleeve on her dress was torn. There was a red spot on the front of the dress. Merle Dawson lay there with her eyes open. A sickle lay a foot away from her outstretched hand.

Luke sat down and pulled his mom's head onto his lap. He gently shook her, trying to get her to talk to him. It was in that position that the first of the neighbors saw Luke when they rode in.

Chapter Two

Luke's father, Prentiss Dawson, was a colonel of
Union Cavalry. He was fighting under Sheridan in the
Shenandoah Valley. Hearing of the death of his wife, he
was granted leave to see to the welfare of his son. Upon
arriving home, the colonel put Luke in the care of his
brother, Seamus, and his wife, Kathleen. They had two
other children, Mary and Ray, so boarding Luke was no
hardship for them.

The colonel sat Luke down and talked to him, "Tell me
what you saw, Lukey. As much as you can remember."

Luke looked at his dad; tears were streaming down
his cheeks. "They had on parts of uniforms, Daddy.
Some were blue, some were gray. I remember one
called the other 'Billy Fred.'" Luke looked at the floor,
then back up angrily at his dad. "I should've gotten the

4

shotgun, Daddy. I should've gotten the shotgun. I could have saved her!" His little fists were doubled up and shaking in frustration.

The big strapping colonel hugged Luke close. Tears were running down his face. "Hush now Luke, there's nothing you could have done. Nothing. Some folks are just no good and that's just the way of things. You didn't even know what was happening." *If you had,* the colonel thought, *you'd have died trying to save her.*

Having settled Luke into his new home, the colonel switched to civilian clothes and went hunting—not for food or sport—but for vengeance. It didn't take him as long as he thought it would to find the men who had slaughtered the woman he loved and terrorized his son. Working primarily on hunches, he trailed 250 miles in five days. From Luke's sketchy description of the clothes and horse colors, the colonel caught up to the three of them on the western border of Arkansas and Missouri.

It was a warm summer morning that June in 1863, and the dawn came early. The birds were chirping and the wildlife was just starting to stir. The area was picturesque, even beautiful. That sentiment was lost on Prentiss Dawson, however, as he'd been crouched there in the bushes half the night watching them, waiting for the right moment. He made his move just before the sun came up over the hill.

Walking forward in a half crouch, he stopped eight feet away from the sleeping men, Spencer cavalry carbine at the ready. He could see a whisky jug on its side along with scraps of food strewn about. The three men were asleep. Two were lying on their backs snoring, and the third was on his side, curled up. He thought about killing them then and there while they slept, but decided against it. When these pieces of human garbage arrived in Sheol, he wanted them to know who sent them there—and why. They had murdered his wife and traumatized his son.

"You three, on your feet!" the colonel called. It came out as more of a growl than a shout.

One man rolled out fast, surprisingly fast, for a man who obviously had a bad hangover. He came up with a pistol in his hand. The colonel was much faster. The shot cracked like thunder. The big .50 caliber bullet of the Spencer caught the man full in the chest and knocked him back five feet. The hole in his chest was large, but the hole in his back, made by the exiting bullet, was cavernous. He lay there, a surprised expression on his face, and a last exclamation on his lips that no one would ever hear. The only sound in the still morning was the rapid cocking of the hammer and the working of the lever to put another cartridge in the chamber. All this happened while echoes of the first round faded away.

The other two, their hands held high, said almost in unison, "Hey now, hey now, that there was old Billy Fred. You didn't have a reason to shoot old Billy Fred."

Billy Fred huh? the colonel thought. *Well, that happened too fast.*

The colonel, with a voice as cold as ice, said, "You two empty your pockets. If you have any weapons, take them out slowly with two fingers."

One, who appeared to still be a little drunk, opened his mouth to say something. He took one look at Prentiss, another at Billy Fred, and closed his mouth with an audible click. The two carefully divested themselves of their pistols. Both men had on a mixture of Confederate and Union uniforms and civilian clothes. They were bleary-eyed from drink. The fastest reaction of the trio had come from their now deceased chum, who lay sprawled on the ground with a hole in him big enough to drive a horse through.

"If you just wanted to rob us, we understand that. That's how we got most of it," the taller of the two said.

Prentiss looked at the pitiful, small pile of loot consisting of his own watch, a gold penknife, two cameos with his wife's name on the back, and a few gold coins. A single tear slid down his cheek, leaving a trail in the dust on his face.

The two were silent as they walked, hands tied behind them, to the big cottonwood tree. They started to cry and beg when the colonel put the rope around their necks. The colonel simply stared at them, eyes as hard as diamonds, saying nothing. "Why are you doin' this?" they asked, begged, pleaded, over and over again.

He threw the other end of the ropes up over a sturdy branch of the tree and tied the ends to his saddle horn. One man had quieted down, fear and resignation alternating in his eyes. The other was blubbering so hard he couldn't speak. Prentiss swung into his saddle and looked back.

"She was my wife," he said simply, and that said it all.

He put his heels to the horse and the two men were slowly dragged into the air where they strangled to death during the next few minutes. He turned around to see their eyes bulging, tongues protruding, and their legs kicking, in a mad danse macabre. The colonel always figured if he was going to kill his man, he should look him in the eye when he did it. When the bodies had finally quit kicking, he sliced the rope from his saddle and rode off, leaving the dead men to the predators. He felt no pleasure in what he'd done, just a grim satisfaction. He wished that he could have taken more time to carry out the execution.

He knew he couldn't bring his wife back, but at least now she could rest in peace. Even though these three dead men wouldn't rest in peace, at least they wouldn't be tearing apart any other families.

The colonel picked up the pistols that the trio had been carrying. He threw the revolvers into the brush. They were Confederate and cheaply made, without recoil shields. He turned the horses loose. It would take two weeks of steady grazing to put them in any kind of riding condition.

He rode back to Kansas to see Luke one more time. When Luke saw the colonel riding up, he ran out to him and threw his arms around the colonel's neck, "Did you get 'em, Daddy? Did you get 'em?"

The colonel looked at Luke and nodded. "You'll never have to worry about them again, Luke. Now I want you to concentrate on learning your studies and the chores around here okay?"

"I will Daddy, I promise."

Then Colonel Prentiss Dawson went back to the war, his war. There was a large skirmish shaping up around a small town in Pennsylvania no one had ever heard of, a place called Gettysburg.

After the Southern surrender at Appomattox Court House, the colonel went back to Kansas, picked up Luke, and began rebuilding his life. He sold his land outside Lawrence and moved west. He settled about thirty miles west of Fort Dodge, in the Arkansas River valley. The ranch was large by Kansas standards, with strategic sections claimed along the Arkansas River, and other sections purchased from the Santa Fe Railroad. With this acquisition and purchase, the colonel controlled over 50,000 acres of good grazing land for raising livestock, mostly cattle, and cropland, for growing corn and wheat. Luke was excited to see his new home and applied all he'd learned about chores.

Chapter Three

Luke's education consisted of the *Bible*, *Pilgrim's Progress*, Blackstone, Shakespeare, various histories, recent and ancient, and mathematics. Many school-teachers were amazed at his knowledge and urged the colonel to send Luke "back East," to school. The colonel would have none of it, saying, "Everything Luke needs to know out of books, he can learn right here, plus a lot more besides." Luke couldn't have agreed more. He loved life with his dad.

Over the next few years, all different sorts of folks would come by to spend the night or to cadge a free meal. The colonel never turned anyone away hungry. He would also give a "beeve" to hungry Indians, usually Cheyenne, Arapaho, and Sioux, as they passed through. It was not surprising that the colonel had no Indian trouble.

One of the cavalry scouts who had served the same time as the colonel during the war was a regular visitor to the ranch, Jim Hickock. Although Jim had served mostly on the western front in Kansas and Missouri, he and the colonel had become acquainted and had a deep mutual respect for each other. Jim cut a dashing figure with his long flowing hair and distinctive mustache. Surprisingly, much of the time, he dressed more like an eastern banker than a frontier marshal. Jim wore a pair of ivory-gripped, engraved, 1851 Navy .36 caliber Colts, butts forward, in a red sash around his waist. Senator Henry Wilson of Massachusetts had presented these beautiful weapons to Jim in 1869, after Jim had scouted for him on a hunting trip. Later to be known as "Wild Bill," Jim took an immediate liking to Luke, and taught him to shoot. He also taught Luke the principle of the fast draw. Use blazing speed to get your gun into action, but hesitate just that fraction of a second to make the first shot true.

Jim also taught Luke all manner of flips, such as the "border shift," which involved flipping an empty pistol up in the air with the right hand to be caught by the left. Simultaneously, he would shift a loaded pistol from the left hand to the right hand, thereby keeping up a contin-ued, accurate fire. Luke practiced this maneuver until he could do it with his eyes closed. Another trick was the "road agents spin," which meant extending the pistols butt forward, as if surrendering, then at the last second rapidly turning them and cocking them. These tricks were later to be made famous by other men.

Once Luke tried a fast draw and then fanned the hammer rapidly with his left hand. The pistol quickly emptied. "Don't ever try that for real Luke, like in a fight," said Jim.

"Why not?" asked Luke.

"Because you almost never hit what you aim at and then you're left with an empty pistol," Jim replied.

Safety instructions were also given to Luke, like: Leave the hammer resting on an empty chamber to avoid accidental firing and always clean your weapons after every use. The most important point was accepting the responsibility of carrying a firearm. No one cared about age. If you carried a weapon, you were presumed capable of using it, and was therefore a deadly threat.

"Don't ever forget that, Luke," Jim emphasized. "If you carry a gun, folks are just naturally going to think you can and will use it."

"That's right, Luke," the colonel added. "Jim and I have seen it happen where a man got shot in the middle of a fracas just for having one." Luke nodded his head thoughtfully.

The colonel gave Luke a pair of Navy Colts, without disclosing their origin, so he could emulate his hero, Wild Bill. The Navy Colt was not named because it was sold to the Navy, but rather for the scene rolled onto the cylinder. This scene depicted an obscure battle between the Texas Navy and some ships from Mexico, May 16, 1843.

The colonel still liked the feel of his big .44 caliber Colt 1860 Army pistol. While this pistol had the same Navy scene on its cylinder, it was named, "the Army," because it was, in fact, sold to the Army. However, Jim, and therefore Luke, preferred the more stream-lined .36 1851 Navy pistol; the grips just seemed more comfortable. Firing with both hands, Luke could regu-larly hit four cans thrown in the air, at the same time, 20 yards away.

Jim, or Wild Bill, as he was getting to be known, would sit at night with the colonel and Luke, and laugh about human nature, how things seemed to stay the same, no matter the time or the place. The three of them would play poker for matchsticks. Luke asked again and again about the science of poker and how to keep a poker face.

"What is all this stuff?" asked Luke.

"Luke, I want to show you how men will sometimes try to 'shade' the odds in their favor," said Jim. With that Jim gave Luke different cheating devices he'd taken off tinhorn gamblers in Ft. Riley, Hays City, and Abilene, places where he had served as a peace officer. Luke was amazed at the array of items. There was everything from simple "shiner" devices, used to peek at the cards, to marked cards. There were also "holdout" contraptions that could deliver a full deck, or a loaded pistol, instantly into the hand of a gambler. "More people have been killed using these things than have been killed in 'honest pursuits' like horse and cattle stealing and bank robbing," Jim would say with a laugh.

Luke and his dad used to travel regularly to Omaha on business. When Luke was fourteen they made yet another trip. While there, they would, whenever possible, take in the performance of Lawrence Barrett, the famous tragedian. Once, while going backstage to pay their respects to Lawrence, they heard not one, but two stentorian voices spouting Shakespeare. One voice was higher than the other. "To be or not to be, that is the question—"

There, in the dressing room, was none other than the "Boy General," George Armstrong Custer. Now a lieutenant colonel of cavalry, Custer was still referred to by his wartime rank of general, out of military courtesy. Custer wore his hair long in the frontier style, as did Jim Hickock. He also wore a long, fringed buckskin jacket. While many thought the fringes were a fancy affectation, they were in fact functional. Each fringe served as an individual rain gutter so water would not stay on the jacket.

"Prent, Prent Dawson you old son-of-a-gun, how have you been? I haven't seen you since you snagged that table for Libby from the McLean house at the village of Appomattox Court House," boomed George Custer.

"Why general, it's great to see you sir. I hope Libby still has that table," said Prentiss.

"Are you kidding? Libby would throw out our bed before she would let go of the table on which the surrender was signed," said Custer. "By the way Prent, after all the saddle leather we've worn out together, can't you call me by the same name you did during the war?"

"All right, Autie." Prentiss laughed. "Say, I'd like you to meet my son, Luke. Luke, this is Major General George Armstrong Custer."

Luke was awestruck. "It–it's an honor sir, General sir," Luke stammered. Luke was in his early teens, but big and strong for his age, yet he marveled at the general's iron grip and the bright gleam in his clear blue eyes.

"Fine boy Prent, fine boy. I wish Libby and I had been blessed with children, but I guess it was not to be," George said with a sigh.

"I wasn't aware you knew each other, Prent," said Lawrence. "However, I should have known. Cavalry under Sheridan was like a big brotherhood."

"I know we didn't have as much fun as being in the infantry like you, Larry, but we did have our moments, didn't we Autie?" Prentiss dryly remarked "What brings you through here, Autie? More Indian trouble?"

"Yes, but not just that," said Custer. "It's the same old story of crooked politicians making corrupt appointments to different bureaus and lining their pockets from the government or the Army, or both. I have to fight a war on two, sometimes three, fronts. I do love life on the plains though, I wouldn't trade it for any-thing. Say, have you seen anything of Jim Hickock? I guess he goes by the name of Wild Bill now. He did a great job of scouting for me back in '67."

"Sure do, see him every six or eight months. He taught Luke to shoot a whole lot better than I can," said Prentiss.

"That's great!" exclaimed Custer. "Son, stay with it, practice every chance you get. Shooting and defending yourself is a skill you can't learn overnight, and you never know when you are going to need it."

On the way home Luke said, "Dad, there seems to me to be a lot of similarity between Jim Hickock and the general."

"How so?" asked Prentiss.

"Well, they both dress kind of fancy in different ways, and both are real good with guns. Also, they both seem like sort of loners in amongst a whole bunch of people," said Luke.

"Good points all," said Prentiss. "There's some-thing else."

"What's that?" asked Luke.

"They are both about the bravest men I have ever seen in battle. Jim Hickock was more behind the Rebel lines than he was ours. And George? Well, in every cav-alry charge I ever saw or heard about him being in-volved in, General Custer was 20 yards in front of everybody, and I mean everybody. Once General Custer had three horses shot out from under him in a single day. He stopped a few spent bullets himself, but was never really wounded."

"They are both real famous men, and I feel privileged to know them," said Luke.

"So do I, son, so do I," said Prentiss.

Chapter Four

A month later, Luke was riding about seven miles north of the ranch looking for stray livestock. Suddenly, up ahead, a man broke from the brush and began limping toward Luke. When he was about 50 yards away, he collapsed. Luke had never seen a Chinaman before, but he knew from his reading that this was probably one, and a pretty beat up one at that. He was wearing black pajama-style clothes which were ragged and torn. It appeared that he had been shot in the leg and severely beaten. His hair was crudely chopped off in the back. Luke rode up and dismounted. He held his canteen of water to the man's mouth. The man gratefully took a drink.

Out of the same brush came a man riding on a mule. A beard adorned his face, silhouetting his hard brown eyes. He was carrying a big rifle. The rifle was the first thing Luke saw. The man had on a torn flannel shirt and filthy bib overalls. An unshaped slouch hat topped off the ensemble. If anything, the mule looked cleaner than the man did.

"Well, sonny, I see you got my Chineeman, I'll just take him from here," the man laughed.

"Your Chinaman?" Luke asked.

"That's right, sonny," said the man, importantly. "I'm from the railroad."

"From the way he's been treated, it doesn't look like you want him back very bad, more like you threw him out—out from a moving train," said Luke.

"Don't get smart with me, sonny, I'll just have to take down your britches and paddle your little behind," the man growled.

Ignoring the insult, Luke asked, "What's he done?"

"Couple of the boys were just funnin' him, that's all," said the man. "They cut off his pigtail and waved it around like an injun scalp. They was laughin' and havin' a good time. He took it serious and beat 'em both up, broke one of their legs. I aim to put this rope on him and drag him back if I have to."

"How did one little Chinaman beat up two big railroad men?" asked Luke.

"I don't know, but it was fast, and he did it, and now I aim to take him back," said the man. "I've had enough talk," he added as he started toward the Chinaman.

"No," said Luke. "You drag him back with a rope, and you'll kill him."

"That's the idea," said the man, as a guffaw erupted from his barrel chest.

The Chinaman looked up at Luke through eyes swollen half shut. Luke left him the canteen and stepped away, conscious of the revolvers in his belt. He walked around to the left side of the mule away from the muzzle of the rifle. It was mid-afternoon, and the shadows were lengthening. Luke's palms were sweaty, so he wiped them on his trousers. His mouth was dry, and he tried to swallow. His blue eyes were narrowed in anticipation of combat, his first. His heart was running faster than any racehorse.

"Now look here boy, no need to get riled," said the man, aware of the change in Luke, and suddenly concil- iatory. "I got papers all legal like, why sure I got papers."

"Let's see them," said Luke.

"Why sure, here they are." The man dismounted keeping his right hand on the comb and hammer of the rifle. As his feet hit the ground, his left hand grabbed the forestock; he cocked the hammer as he turned. His grin exposed tobacco-stained teeth; curiously, almost the same color as his brown beard. As the man turned, he leveled the rifle at Luke.

As fast as he had ever done in practice, faster maybe, Luke drew and fired one of his Colts. He hit the man in the shoulder thinking that it would end the argument. He was wrong. The man flinched and swore, then brought up the rifle again. Luke fired twice more, this time hitting his opponent in the cheek and the eye. The man fell over backward into the mule. The mule shied away, kicking up little puffs of dust in agitation. The man lay on his back, arms akimbo. One eye was open, the other closed. Luke took one look, then turned away and retched and retched again, until he could retch no more.

Later, Luke put the Chinaman up on the mule. For his small stature, the Chinaman was surprisingly heavy. He tied the Chinaman onto the mule, put it on a lead rope, and rode very slowly back to the ranch house. It was dusk by the time they got there. The sun shone a beautiful late-day gold. Seeing two animals riding up, the colonel came out to have a look. By this time, Luke looked sicker than the Chinaman.

This was Luke's introduction to Sing Loo.

"Get 'em inside, boys. Have a look at that leg. Come on in the other room son, have a seat."

Luke walked in and collapsed into one of the over-stuffed chairs with his head down, looking disconsolate.

"Tell me what happened, Luke," said the colonel gently.

Luke told him about the incident, leaving nothing out. When he got through, he looked bleakly at the colonel. "It wasn't like shooting tin cans, Dad, it was awful, I didn't know what else I could do, I had no choice."

"None that I can see. I'll have Pete and a couple others go out and have a look at daylight. In the meantime, you better have a few sips of brandy, and try to get a good night's sleep."

As Luke thought about it later, second-guessing himself, he wished he had tried to get the drop on the man and maybe avoided bloodshed. He had tried to just wound him instead, and that was foolish too. Jim Hickock had said more than once, "Any time you get mad enough at a man to shoot him, you might as well kill him. He's not going to think any more kindly of you for having just shot him." Luke wasn't sure he totally agreed with that sentiment, but in this instance Wild Bill was right on the money.

Pete, the foreman, and two of the hands, Rowdy and Tex, rode back in about mid-morning, still talking quietly among themselves. Peter Ryan, late of the Union Army, was a big second-generation Irishman. He had served under Colonel Prentiss Dawson from Bull Run to Appomattox as his top sergeant. He stood six and a half feet tall and weighed over 260 pounds. People never argued with him when they were sober, and not often when drunk. His hair was dark brown and his eyes an emerald green. His eyes were light when joking, and the color of deep marble when stirred to anger. On his left cheek was a four-inch scar, a souvenir of the Battle of Yellow Tavern.

"It was just like Luke said, colonel, the man was stretched out. He had one in the shoulder, and two in the head, pretty darn good shootin' if you ask me."

"What did you do with him?" the colonel asked.

"We scratched a hole in the ground and tossed him in. Didn't say any words over him though, didn't figure he deserved them trying to sucker a kid thata way. I brought this back," Pete said, holding out the rifle. "The hammer was on full cock when I found it, and there was a cartridge in the chamber. It was a close call."

Feeling detached, Luke wondered at his own instinctive reactions. How could he appreciate all those lessons from Wild Bill and yet feel so bad?

Chapter Five

As near as anyone could tell, Sing Loo was some sort of philosopher or thinker. He had come from China to make his fortune and had ended up on a railroad gang. The big tracks had been laid back in 1869, connecting the Union Pacific and the Central Pacific Railroads at Promontory Point, Utah. However, they needed a lot of maintenance and shoring up in places, and new branches were being built.

Sing Loo was a good cook, who could also do heavy work with the best of them. He was small but that did not mean that he was weak. Quite the contrary. When he was very young he was taught philosophy, and along with that, he was taught to use his whole being to defend himself. His queue or pigtail, was a large part of his being. When the two big Irishmen grabbed him and cut off his queue, Sing Loo was enraged. He first disarmed them, much to their surprise, then proceeded to beat them up. He broke one of their legs and bruised them both beyond recognition. At that point a whole group of "gandy dancers" came after Sing Loo with axe handles. He was beaten up pretty good, and no one felt like stopping. Sing Loo managed to get away, but not before he took a bullet in the leg for company. The man on the mule had shot Sing Loo, and would have done so again if Luke had not been there when the man caught up to him.

It was rough, but effective surgery, to get the slug out of Sing Loo's leg. The colonel had done it many times during the war and had not lost his skill. He even used clean utensils, something rarely heard of during the Civil War. The healing process went fast and Sing Loo was up and around within the week.

To say that Sing Loo felt an obligation to Luke would be putting it mildly. Luke had saved his life and Sing Loo felt honor-bound to repay him, although he was amazed when he found out how young Luke was. While Luke, on his part, was glad to have been able to help, he did not view the situation in the same way Sing Loo did.

Sing Loo created a problem by following Luke everywhere he went. He compounded the problem by not being very good around animals and trying to help too much.

Once when Luke started to pick up a bucket of water, Sing Loo grabbed the bucket and trailed after Luke trying to anticipate what he might need. The mule he had ridden to the ranch eyed Sing Loo and began twitching his ears. Just as Sing Loo was passing behind him, the mule lashed out with both hooves. Sing Loo was knocked tail over teakettle and rolled in the straw, corn shucks, and new dung. He came up sputtering, soaking wet with his dignity bruised. The bucket, now bent beyond recognition, was still in his hand. Even though Luke had wanted to learn some Chinese, he wasn't sure he wanted to learn the meaning of those particular words that came out of Sing Loo.

Another time, Sing Loo roped a horse so he could saddle him for Luke. The rope fell over the horse's chest and before he could tighten it, Sing Loo was given a ride around the corral on his backside. The watching ranch hands exploded in mirth much to the dismay of Sing Loo.

Finally, Luke said, "Sing Loo, it takes time to understand the workings of animals. You don't have to rush it. There is one thing I would appreciate your help with, though."

"What is that?"

"You have a style of fighting that can overcome bigger men, and many men. I would like to know about it and learn to use it. Is that possible?"

"Yes Luke, it is possible. But first you have to do something."

"All right, what?"

"You have to forget all about the American way of fighting. Only a fool fights just with fists. That can hurt your hand. Chinese men fight with their fists, yes, but they also use fingers, thumbs, elbows, the head, knees, feet, legs, even hips. Chinese men have no guns. Everything can be a weapon. Look here, what do you see?" Sing Loo pointed to the ground.

"I see corn shucks, some straw, and a pile of dung."

"No, you see weapons."

"Weapons?"

"Yes, weapons. Corncobs can be shoved in the throat. Many corncobs can be put in a sack to make a club. Straw bound together and shoved in the face hurts. Dung, shoved in eyes, can blind for a short time. Also, it will let you know the enemy is coming, because you can smell 'em."

"A joke? Sing, I can't believe it, you actually made a joke."

"Heh, heh," chortled Sing. "One more thing, the most important. When you fight, fight to win, do not fight for fun."

Thus began a rigorous training program for Luke.

They strung three large bags of grain from the rafters in the barn in the shape of a large triangle. What Sing Loo didn't know about animals, he more than made up for in his fighting skills. Luke learned all manner of kicks, punches, feints, pivots, and throws. Sing Loo would push and pull all three bags at the same time, making Luke duck, dodge, and hit.

"You have to hit the opponent hard, because he can hit back, while the bag does not hit back. Remember, always use the opponents' strengths against them. If he pushes, you don't push, you pull! If he pulls, you don't pull, you push! So if he's a big man, he will have a big fall."

Luke kept up his practice on a daily basis or whenever time allowed. Sometimes Luke and Sing Loo would work out in practice sessions. They would always pull their punches, but the activity could get spirited. While he was only a little over five feet tall, Sing Loo could flip Luke into a pile of hay. A little later, Luke returned the favor with a stomach throw. Sing Loo's only response was, "Ah, good."

The days seemed to go by very quickly. Gradually Sing Loo had taken over the duties of cook. This was a task he was well suited for and that the others were very glad to let him have. He thought of many different ways to cook the same food and made it very appetizing. The colonel and everybody else drew the line when Sing Loo buried some eggs in a pile of straw and wanted to dig them up and serve them thirty days later. While they might have liked those eggs in China, over here just the idea of them could make the boys sick to their stomach.

Chapter Six

Luke grew over the next couple of years. He could do the work of any ranch hand and more. He never asked for, nor was he given, any slack by the colonel, Pete, or anyone else. His incredible shooting skills won him a healthy respect from the hands, old and new alike. Even those hands who thought they were pretty "salty" and good "pistoleers" gave Luke a wide berth when it came to shooting for money. For his part, Luke didn't let his firearm skill go to his head. He just tried to improve for the next time he would see Wild Bill. Jim's visits however, were becoming more infrequent.

On his last visit Jim said, "By golly, I answer more now to Bill than I do my own name."

"Ah, the price of fame, Jim," said the colonel with a laugh.

"Luke, you really are skilled now in the use of firearms," Jim observed. "It's good to put on exhibitions at any opportunity. Showing your skill will make the other fellow just that much more reluctant to take you on. What you have to look out for is the sneaky little cowards who will try to back-shoot you."

"I'll do my best, Jim," Luke replied. "But it sounds like I need eyes in the back of my head."

"That's not a bad idea," Jim answered.

If Luke ever did get to feeling too good about himself, all he had to do was have another workout with Sing Loo. It was real humbling to be thrown all over the barn by a little man barely five feet tall, and ten years older than he was.

One day when Luke was almost eighteen, a young fellow named Henry Bowen came in riding the "grubline." He didn't look particularly down on his luck with his custom boots, canvas riding pants, muslin shirt, and high-crowned Stetson hat. On his hips he wore two modern Colt single action pistols, tied down with rawhide strips. He looked about twenty-three, but could have been a couple of years on either side of that. He was almost six feet tall, compact in build with sandy hair and light blue eyes that hinted at a devilish streak.

The Circle D, Dawson's brand, had a reputation for never turning anyone away, and was happy to feed him. Over dinner he casually asked if any of the boys liked to shoot. He then added, to make it interesting, maybe they could put a little bit of money on the outcome.

A couple of the hands snickered, and looked at each other out of the corners of their eyes. Pete, keeping a poker face said, "What did you have in mind?"

"Well, I don't have a lot of money but, if some of you boys want to get up a pot, we can all shoot for it or, I'll just shoot against any one in the bunch of you," said Henry.

"Well, the most shiftless rider we got is old Luke here, so we let him do most of the shooting of varmints. He's pretty good on snakes if they're close up, and you give him two or three tries."

Luke had just swallowed a mouthful of coffee, and began coughing and laughing when Pete finished talking. Luke stood up and held out his hand, "Hi, I'm Luke Dawson."

Henry Bowen stood up and held out his own hand. "Heard of you," he said simply. Luke merely nodded his head, knowing now that the entire preamble was over.

"All right boys, without further ado, let's adjourn to the shooting range. How do you want to do it, Henry? It seems like you've done this before," Pete said, with a slight edge to his voice, his eyes the color of deep emerald.

Henry, taking note of the edge said, "If it's all right with you, we each choose two kinds of a game. The other fellow shoots first on the game not of his choosing."

"Yeah, you've done this before."

"Aw heck, look, I don't want any hard feelings, I'm

just looking for a little fun. You folks were kind enough to feed me, and I hear Luke here is pretty good."

Stepping in, Luke said, "Hey that's fine, let's have some fun. What can it hurt, except that I might lose a little money. Gather up some tin cans."

"And a couple of silver dollars," said Henry.

"And a couple of dimes," Luke added.

Henry was feeling pretty confident up to the mention of the dimes. At that point the expression on his face turned quizzical.

It was a nice spring afternoon, not too hot, with a slight breeze blowing from the southwest. They all walked behind the bunkhouse facing away from the sun and the livestock. Luke still used his Navies and Henry his single-action, all Colt products.

The colonel, hearing about the contest, sauntered out from the main house and stood at the back of the group of men, saying nothing.

Henry won the toss of the coin so he got to pick the first event. He chose drawing and firing at a silver dollar thrown in the air. He hoped that the pressure of the quick firing of the first event might rattle Luke, and affect him for the later ones.

Luke stood easy, arms crossed left over right. Pete threw the silver dollar high in the air as he had thrown hundreds of similar objects for Luke before. Luke drew and fired his Navy in one fluid motion. After being struck, the dollar flew higher and Luke fired again. This time the dollar spun downward after being hit and landed in the ground with a hard thunk.

"Good thing nobody was standing under that, they would have lost a toe," joked Mike, one of the hands.

Pete threw another silver dollar for Henry. Henry's arm swept down and came up with his pistol firing. He hit the dollar on his first shot, but sent it farther out, and with his second shot, he missed.

"Tough luck," said Luke.

"Yeah," groused Henry.

Luke chose stationary peach cans as targets at sixty yards for his first event. Pete lined up six cans three feet apart; there would be no luck involved here.

"If I wanted a rifle shoot, I'd have unlimbered my Winchester," said Henry, as he peered at the cans in the distance.

"I find it's good practice, in case I'm ever caught without my rifle," Luke answered.

Henry drew his pistol, and standing square to the targets took six carefully aimed shots. He missed the first one. After readjusting his aim, he got the next three. The fifth can he missed, and the sixth only rocked as he grazed the outside.

"Not bad," said Luke.

"How are you going to count that sixth can? I didn't really hit it."

"If you'd been shooting at someone, they'd have felt it." Luke said.

Pete made the call. "We'll count it as a hit. It's not

going to matter anyhow." Henry looked quickly at Pete, to see if he was kidding. Pete kept a stone face. Luke, looking over the back of Henry's shoulder at Pete, smiled and shook his head.

Luke drew his Navy Colt, and stood in the classic off-hand stance taught to him by his father and Wild Bill. His 'feet were at a forty-five-degree angle to the line, his left hand behind his back. Taking slow, controlled breaths, he leveled the pistol above the target, and then brought it down. His first shot was right in the center of the can. The can went straight back then flipped in the air. The next three shots went exactly the same way; the cans hit dead center. Luke's lighter caliber pistol made a cracking sound instead of the boom of Henry's .44-40. On the fifth can, Luke hit to the left of center, spinning it around behind the sixth. Luke shot the sixth can in the top, knocking it back end over end, into the fifth can. The sound they made rolling together was like the start of a shivaree.

"Did you do that on purpose? Whoa, I'll just bet you did!" exclaimed Henry. "I thought I was pretty good, but I've never seen anything like that."

"It doesn't work all the time," said Luke.

"It surely did that time!" Henry again exclaimed.

While they had seen Luke shoot many times before, Pete, Mike, Rowdy, Tex, and the rest of the hands still openly marveled at his skill.

Henry was shucking empty shells out of his pistol when he glanced over at Luke, who was trading empty cylinders for full ones in his Colts. While Luke was placing percussion caps on the cylinder nipples, Henry ventured an opinion.

"I know I got no call to be telling you anythin' about firearms Luke, but how come you don't have something that takes a cartridge instead of powder wrapped in paper? Maybe at least get those Navies converted to cartridge?"

"You got a good point, Henry. I guess I just like the feel of the Navy, and haven't gotten around to getting them converted."

"Heft this, Luke." Henry extended one of his single-action Colts to Luke.

"It does have a nice feel to it. I think the grip is the same size as the Navy. Maybe I'll have to try a couple of these," said Luke "What do you want to do for the next game?"

"How about if we go blindfolded." Henry laughed. "No? Then we'll just have to play walk the can."

"How's that?"

"We start off with two pistols drawn, and walk the can starting at ten yards until both guns are empty. The rule is that you have to hit the can every time."

"Sounds good to me." Luke said.

Luke crouched and started off firing with both hands. His pistols made a sound like a continuous roll of thunder. The can jumped, whirled, and sang as it whipped through the air. When the can finally came to rest it looked more like a sieve than anything else.

Next came Henry's turn. His shot could be heard individually. While maybe not quite as fast, his performance was equal to Luke's.

"Looks like a tie," Luke observed.

"'Bout as close as I'm going to get to one," added Henry.

"Okay, my choice on the last one," declared Luke. "We put a dime on the back of our left hand, then we draw and hit it as it's dropped to the ground. No throwing it up in the air."

"And I get to try this crazy stunt first. Aren't I the lucky one," Henry said. And try Henry did, with a clean miss.

Luke placed the dime carefully on the back of his hand, the seated liberty coin poised for the drop. The drop of the hand and the sound of the pistol were simultaneous. What was left of the dime came to rest about twenty feet away.

Pete and the rest of the hands whooped and laughed. The colonel allowed himself a smile, which slowly spread into a proud grin.

"Well, Luke," said Henry "I purely did get an education today, and it only cost me fifteen dollars." Henry put three five-dollar gold pieces, also known as half-eagles, into Luke's hand.

"Why shucks Henry, I appreciate the company and the competition. Say listen, what brought you all the way out here in the first place? It wasn't just the good food was it?"

"No, I guess you know why. I'd heard about you and wanted to see how good you really were. I guess I found out. In fact, you're the best I've ever seen, let alone shot against."

"Say, Henry," said Pete, who obviously had had a change of heart, "you looking for a job?"

"Not right now, I've got a few things to get settled in Dodge, but I surely do appreciate the offer, Pete."

"Ah, you know, I thought I would let somebody spell old Luke from having to shoot all them snakes."

Everybody laughed, even Henry.

"If the offer's still open in a month, I'd be proud to work for the Circle D."

"Why, we'd be proud to have you, Henry. Some of the boys just drift off when winter sets in, and there's not a lot to do, but if you're interested, you can have a year-round job," Pete said.

"What does the job pay?"

"We pay thirty dollars a month and food. You can keep your own horse and we'll feed him. You can use him for the general work, or cut one out of the remuda, your call. One other thing, if there is any shootin', we pay double for fighting wages."

"Does that happen?"

"Sometimes. Not often, but sometimes."

"That's okay. I'll be back inside a month, and then, whatever happens, I ride for the brand." Henry mounted his paint and with a casual wave rode back toward Dodge City.

"I like him," said Luke.

"Aw, you just like the color of his gold." Pete chuckled. "But, yes, I like him too."

The colonel walked up. "Good shooting, son."

"Thanks, Dad."

"Come on up to the house. I want to show you something." They walked side by side, and with their similar builds, they could have been brothers. Luke was just over six feet tall and weighed 190 pounds. The colonel was just a bit heavier and in his temples had a touch of gray. He looked like a mature version of Luke.

Luke walked into the main room and sat down. The colonel went into the back and came out carrying some firearms. Luke's eyes got wide. "What's all this, Dad?"

"This, or rather these, are your birthday presents. I figured I'd give them to you now rather than wait. The Colt single actions are the same as the ones you saw Henry using. The caliber .44-40 is the same in this Winchester Model '73. That means you can use the same cartridge for all the weapons. These are the finest weapons made today. Oh sure, there are some that shoot farther, but none that will get out the rate of fire that these can." On the sides of the pistols and the rifle was engraved "Luke Dawson" and a big "Circle D."

"Golly, thanks Dad. This means an awful lot to me coming from you. I'll never forget this. Especially with those inscriptions. I can't wait to try them."

"I know son, I know. Here's something else, I had these holsters made specially for you. They hold your pistols at the same angle that you carry them now, in your belt. Wild Bill likes his sash, but you do a lot of riding, and I thought the holsters might be more comfortable."

Luke got up and walked over to the table. He took out his Navy Colts and put them on the table. As he picked up the holster set he said, "These are as nice as anything I have ever seen." He strapped them on, and felt the heft of the rig. "They are a little bit heavier than the Navies, but definitely something I can get used to. Can I try them out now?"

"Don't you think the sunlight is fading?"

"Aw c'mon, Dad, you know if you can see it, you can shoot it. You taught me that from when you were in the Army."

"You're going to have a lot of guns to clean tonight."

Out they went, Luke proud as a peacock with his new weapons. Luke performed the tin can walk again, with the same results. Then he practiced drawing, and found the holsters, hardened like iron, even easier to draw from than his belt. Luke had fired lever action Winchesters before, of course, but this was nice since it was the same caliber as the Colts and besides, it had seventeen shots. The rifle was accurate, with a little elevation, to about 400 yards. "What a package, thanks, Dad!"

"Happy birthday, son."

Chapter Seven

Two weeks later, Luke and Sing Loo decided to drive the buckboard into Dodge City to pick up some supplies. Dodge City had been founded a few years before in 1872 as a companion to nearby Ft. Dodge. Ft. Dodge was built to protect that section of the Santa Fe Trail in 1865. Dodge City was not yet the cattle town it would soon become. It was however, the hub of much trade activity including the sale of buffalo hides. The Santa Fe Railroad had shortly before established a shipping point on the outskirts of town. The colonel had the idea to buy lean cattle, longhorns and mixed breeds from Texans, and then fatten them up on the rich Kansas range grass. When they were nice and plump, he would drive them in to Dodge City and sell them for a nice profit. He envisioned a profit of about 50–75% after costs.

While the ranch could grow about everything they needed in the way of foodstuffs, it was still nice to pick up seasonings, canned fruit, and coffee, and to stock up on ammunition. Luke took his new weapons with him to get familiar with them and just in case they were needed.

They left before dawn to get a good start on the day. The weather was cool, but it would soon turn hot, as the day progressed. The thirty-mile drive to Dodge was un-eventful. The road, if it could be called that, was on the north side of the Arkansas River along mostly level ground. It was a trail well traveled first by Indians, then by buffalo hunters, both now a dying breed, although neither group knew it yet.

The Indians however, showed plenty of fight to maintain their way of life. In fact, the biggest Indian battles were yet to come. The law of supply and demand motivated the hunters, and buffalo hides were all the rage. While the Indian could use every part of a buffalo, including the hoof, the white buffalo hunter would take only the hide, the tongue, and sometimes the hump, the most tender meat parts. It would infuriate the Indians when they saw thousands of rotting buffalo carcasses on the prairie. That was just one bone of contention between the two groups of people.

Another, and perhaps the biggest area of conflict, was the concept of the ownership of land. Plains Indians were nomadic. They would travel with the seasons or where the hunting was good. The idea of permanent towns, or fenced-off land, was completely foreign to them. Conflict was inevitable. Broken treaties, corrupt Indian agents, and suppliers of inferior goods, all helped to stir the cauldron of trouble.

Luke and Sing Loo met two small groups of Comanche with women and children, but Luke's armament and an empty wagon made the idea of pursuing plunder not worth the risk.

When the wind was right, as it was that day, they could smell Dodge City a long time before they saw it. Sing Loo drove the wagon into Dodge City about 9:30 in the morning. The town was just starting to stir. Some of the citizens were still drunk from the night before. Others were nursing gigantic hangovers, the kind they could only get from "snakehead" whisky. There were hotels and saloons with pretentious names like the Lady Gay, the Long Branch, the Lone Star, Hoover's, to name a few, and one, Grant, and one, Lee, to express other sentiments. All any of them consisted of was usually long narrow buildings with a false clapboard front extending over the roof. This false front was thought to be a help in advertising, perhaps not the first time the term was used, and certainly not the last. The floors were more often than not packed dirt. The street was dusty and full of chuckholes, and when it was wet, it became a quagmire.

Driving through the streets, their nostrils were assailed

by the stench of dung, dirt, vomit, stale whisky, and decaying buffalo hides. Sing Loo pulled the buckboard up in front of the building aptly named General Store. As they walked into the store, they found it had wooden floors. They were pleasantly surprised by the smells: New leather, dried apples, cloves, tobacco, and coffee. Wafting out from the back was also the faint odor of gun oil.

Silas Barrett was the owner of the General Store. He was a medium-sized fellow with a large belly, a completely bald head, and a full black beard. He had been wounded fighting for the North in the Civil War and, as a result, his left arm was shorter than his right. "Hello, Luke, if you didn't look so much like your daddy, I don't think I'd have recognized you. Why you're almost full-grown."

"Hi, Silas, it's good to see you."

"Say, I see you got those new firearms, how do you like them?"

"They're great! The balance in the pistols is just like my Navies and the rifle is real accurate."

"I had to order them special from Schuyler, Hartley, and Graham out of New York because of the engraving. Your dad wanted it professionally done, not put on by some jeweler. It took the better part of a year to get them. Colt and Winchester are way backed up on their orders. I imagine you'll want some .44-40 ammunition?"

"Yeah, a few cases. Dad's going to be sorry he got me these new irons." Luke laughed, and so did Silas.

"You have new spices?" asked Sing Loo.

"Sure, Sing, right there in the corner. Go ahead and pick out what you need. We'll tally it up as you go."

Luke carried out several cases of .44-40 shells along with some other types of ammunition. Sing Loo selected many kinds of spices and several boxes of canned peaches, the cowboy's favorite. They would take a knife and poke a hole in the top and drink off the juice, then eat the peaches—pure heaven when they were out on a dusty range. Luke paused to admire a new shirt, then went to the side and picked up a stout wooden box of Arbuckle's coffee.

As he walked toward the front of the store, he heard a great commotion out in front. When he walked out the door, he heard loud, raucous laughter from a group of men. There was Sing Loo shouting and probably swearing in Chinese, but with good reason. A big buffalo hunter had hold of his queue and was swinging him around and around. Between centrifugal force and the length of his queue, Sing Loo could do nothing. He was reaching back and making little swipes to no avail, only provoking more laughter.

"Hey, little man, we're gonna twirl you so fast your eyes'll roll round," one of them called. They all laughed, and began taking savage swings with their fists at Sing Loo as he went past them, and sometimes they connected with a sharp thud.

There were four of them. They looked as if they could have been brothers, and were at least all related by blood. All were big men and very strong. The one whirling Sing Loo was doing so with just one hand. None of them had shaved in six months. They wore homespun shirts, canvas overalls, and work boots. They had come in to Dodge City from the prairie three days before with a full load of buffalo hides, which they sold to Wright and Rath. They were still celebrating their good fortune. Two were half-drunk from the night before, and two were sober enough to be just cussed mean.

Silas looked out and exclaimed, "It's the Slonikers!"

Luke dropped the Arbuckle's on the front stoop with a loud crash. Temporarily forgetting everything he had learned from Sing Loo, he charged out into the street. Just as Sing Loo was going around again, Luke ran up and gave the man holding him a tremendous kick in the backside. The man fell forward sprawling on all fours and released Sing Loo who then rolled, and kept rolling out of the way. Sing Loo got up on wobbly legs and made his way over to the buckboard. The attention of all four was now firmly centered on Luke. The morning had given way to a warm noontime sun. The stench of the street was becoming even more pungent.

Luke's head cleared; some of the rage had dissipated. Now he felt more of a cold fury directed at these louts. The one who received the kick stood up, his dignity injured, and started forward. "Well, well, looks like we got us a white knight. Maybe we'll just have to show him who his betters are." Luke put up his fists and waited.

The man started forward, hands held loose. Luke

feinted toward the man's face with his left hand. The man instinctively reached up to grab Luke's arm, intending to grapple and chew, rather than fight with his fists. The act of reaching up left him open down below. Luke set himself, quickly pulled back his left arm, and fired two rapid, powerful right fists into the man's midsection. All the months and years of training on heavy grain sacks showed in the strength and force of the blows. The man's breath left him with a whoosh, and with a groan he bent over at the waist. Stepping up, Luke threw a solid left hook into the man's ear, and heard a satisfying smack. Then Luke threw a straight right into the man's nose, and felt an even more satisfying crunch. Blood began to flow from the shattered nose. Luke stepped around to the left side of the man and with the edge of his right hand hit the man on the left side of the neck at his carotid artery. The man went down moaning.

Sing Loo had recovered from his vertigo and pummeling, and from the ringside seat of the buckboard was cheering and coaching Luke. "Luke, Luke don't just use fists, you can hurt your hand—ah, that was a good hit."

Leaving their fallen companion, the other three fanned out and worked their way in. Two of them went one way, and one ran the other, behind Luke, and took a wild swing at the back of his head.

"Luke, you better duck—ah, I bet that hurt," Sing Loo said with a wince.

Luke did duck enough to make the blow only a glancing one, but it still did hurt. Luke didn't know if he was madder at the men, or at Sing Loo, who was so obviously enjoying himself.

The man from behind Luke closed in, swinging roundhouses left and right. Luke dodged and ducked and then reached out and grabbed the man's shirt and belt, while he pivoted. At the same time, he turned away and straightened up. Now, using all his leverage, he had the man's body up in the air balancing him overhead, then Luke slammed him into the rear wheel of the buckboard. The man's head made a sickening whack as it hit the rim. He lay there crumpled and still, like a half-full grain sack with lumps in it.

"Oh, that was nice," said Sing Loo.

Luke whirled around to meet the other two. One of them was advancing with a wicked skinning knife held low. They were so close, Luke didn't know if he had enough time to unthong a pistol. A can of peaches flew by Luke's face and hit the man with the knife right square in the forehead with a loud thwack. The man dropped to his knees and fell forward like a poleaxed ox.

"The knife was not nice. I hope I did not hurt the peaches," said Sing Loo, "The colonel might not like it."

The last man ran at Luke in a bull rush, arms extended. Luke grabbed the insides of the man's arms with both hands and rocked backward on his left foot. Luke put his right foot crossways in the man's stomach and let the man's momentum carry him up and over.

Luke rolled onto his back carrying the man with him. At the top of the throw Luke pushed up with his right foot and threw the man high up in the air. Rather than pull the man's arms in and break his fall, as he would do in practice with Sing Loo, Luke left him out there to fall straight down on his head. The man let out a strangled cry on the way down. The effect when the man hit the ground was not unlike that of being hit by a piledriver. Only this pile needed just one drive, and was lying there unconscious, his head twisted painfully to the side. The man lay partially submerged in the filth of the street, with his mouth full of dirt, blending in with the surroundings.

"Ah, good," said Sing Loo.

By this time, several spectators had gathered. Silas had walked out on the front walk, a Colt single action in his hand, and a smile on his face. This crew had given him trouble before. There were also several buffalo hunters, some girls, and local gamblers, watching the proceedings with varying levels of amusement. It seemed the Slonikers were well known, and had few friends in Dodge City.

Two men from Wells Fargo were also there; Jerome Puddington, and Andrew Lewis. The first man, Jerome, was a small thin man in his early forties. He wore a black suit and a black bow tie; his hat was a black bowler. He had a pair of glasses folded carefully in his pocket. Jerome was out of the San Francisco headquarters office, and checked on Wells Fargo operations throughout the company. Jerome had lively blue eyes set deep in a narrow face. He had an earnest air about him that might make some men underestimate his razor sharp mind. Few would have thought that Jerome had once been a rider for Russell, Majors, and Waddel, the ones who had formed the Pony Express. Wells Fargo later bought them out. In his leather-lined pocket, he carried a new, small, .38 caliber five-shot-double-action pistol by Forehand and Wadsworth. The pistol was not much good beyond 15 feet, but that was enough.

The second man, Andrew Lewis was a big, stocky man who still looked like the former teamster driver he had been. Andrew had a florid face and kind brown eyes. He wore black frontier pants, a blue flannel shirt, and low cut boots. On his head he seldom wore anything but his Stetson. Carried high on his hip was a Colt 1860 .44 caliber Army revolver converted from percussion to cartridge.

Andrew and Jerome were there to scout out the possibility of a new Wells Fargo location. They saw Dodge City as a town rough even by frontier standards, and welcomed the fight both as confirmation of their judgment and as an entertaining diversion.

"That kid can sure hit," said Andrew.

"Yes, but look how he uses his whole body throwing those ruffians around. I've never seen anything like that," remarked Jerome.

"Look at that Chinese man hopping around and yelling, you'd think he was in the fight," Andrew exclaimed.

"Oh, I think he's got more to do with this than meets the eye," said Jerome. About that time, the peach can went sailing and clobbered one of the Slonikers. "See what I mean? I also think that man taught the kid an awful lot of what he is doing."

"Well, somebody did, that's for sure, 'cause I've never seen anything like it either." The fight had just ended, with the last Sloniker pretending to be a one-legged stilt in the street.

"That was quick, real quick," said Jerome.

Suddenly a shot rang out. Not so rare for later on in the day, but unusual at this time. Andrew reached for his .44, and Jerome put his hand inside his pocket, as they both crouched and looked around warily.

"If you're going to pull something like that, you face a man straight away, you gutless, yellow coward!" The voice of Henry Bowen rang out loud and clear down the street. He had fired a shot in front of the first Sloniker, the one with the broken nose. The man had recovered enough to go and get his big Sharps .50 caliber sporting rifle, a gun used for hunting buffalo. He was stalking Luke from behind, when Henry spotted him and fired just in front of his feet.

Luke turned, drawing both his Colts as he did, and faced the man 40 yards away. He cocked and pointed his pistol square at the man's chest, hand steady, breathing fast, but getting more controlled with each breath. "Go ahead," Luke said, "Bring that rifle barrel around, let's see if you're faster than a .44-40 slug."

The man was carrying the Sharps rifle across his chest hunter style, and had been swinging it around, preparing to take a shot at Luke when Henry fired in front of him. Blood from his nose was leaking down his beard and onto his rifle. Seeing the steady Colt in Luke's hand, he thought he might better have business somewhere else. He started to back up, "No, No, I reckon not, not this time, at least."

"Hold it!" Luke said in a cutting voice. The man stopped.

"Put the rifle down!"

"What? No, I mean, it's a new gun. You mean down here in this dirt? No, I just bought it." The man whined, still leaking blood on the weapon. The Sharps was his prized possession and was cleaner than the man.

"Drop it or use it!"

The man hesitated only a second, wiped the dripping blood off the rifle with his sleeve, then with a sigh put the rifle carefully, almost lovingly, on the ground. He then backed away off to the side, hopeful that he could retrieve his weapon a little later.

Luke eyed the Sloniker backing away. He shifted his glare to the Sharps. Luke's first shot split the buttstock, and the second shattered it. The third shot shattered the forestock. The fourth shot hit the back of the hammer, breaking the action and driving the hammer into the firing pin. This in turn exploded the cartridge in the chamber that sent a big caliber .50 slug plowing into the dirt, right beside the yelping Sloniker. The remaining shots were dedicated to making the rifle into a use-less pile of scrap. It was not lost on any of the specta-tors that Luke was firing very fast and didn't miss once—at 40 yards. Henry could have told them that Luke could do the same thing at 60 yards. The echoes of the shots died away. The cloud of smoke gradually cleared, revealing a horrified Sloniker looking at the re-mains of his beautiful Sharps. The acrid smell of smoke still hung in the air and mingled with the stench of the street.

"Kid can shoot too!" Jerome exclaimed.

"Sure can," Andrew agreed.

Luke stood in the middle of the street, ejecting empty cartridge casings and reloading fresh shells into his pistols. This was a major point he had learned early on: Always reload quickly, you don't know who, or what, might be coming next.

Henry Bowen strolled over while he was reloading his own pistol. "Hi there, Luke, you are some kind of wildcat, taking on four of them like that—might not have been too healthy. Of course, you can thank Sing Loo for taking out one of them. He ought to be pitching for a baseball team. That old boy he hit with the peach can is still resting peacefully, there in the road."

"Henry! I think I better thank you too! If it hadn't been for you I might have had a hole in me big enough to drive a wagon through. Between you and Sing, my back was pretty well covered, fortunately. Any time you need a favor, ask."

"How about a couple?"

"Name 'em."

"Well I think my business is taken care of here in Dodge, I thought I'd ride on out to the Circle D."

"Henry, you were on the payroll from the time you fired that shot. I think I can square it with Pete. What else?"

"Do you think you can teach me to fight the way you just did? I mean, using those throws and making people flying all over the place?"

Luke laughed, and Sing Loo, who was standing nearby started to chuckle.

"Did I say something funny?" Henry asked, a puzzled expression on his face.

"No, no, it's not you Henry, it's just that I asked Sing Loo the same question two years ago. I haven't begun to learn what he knows, but sure, I think Sing would be happy to show you what he can, wouldn't you, Sing?"

"Ah, you bet. It will be much more fun to throw two men 'stead of one."

Chapter Eight

Luke observed Sheriff Tom LeBeau walking down the street. He looked, Luke thought, full of himself to make up for a lack of confidence. He was wearing custom boots, brown buck cord pants, a yellow muslin fabric gambler's shirt, and a Stetson hat. On his hip he carried, low and tied down, a Colt .45 caliber single action pistol. He was about the same size as Luke, but his brown eyes were close together, and darted furtively back and forth. His cheeks were sallow, and his skin pale, indicating a preference for the indoors.

"Well, what's going on here? Sounded like a range war."

Silas tucked his pistol behind his apron and spoke up. "It's those Slonikers again, Sheriff, only this time they're on the north side of Front Street, bothering my customers. That riffraff is supposed to stay on the south side of the tracks. You know that, why don't you make them stay there?"

"Aw, I can't be every place at once. What happened anyway?"

"Those four decided to make sport of Sing Loo, and Luke here got mad."

"It does appear that he got a mite peeved," said the sheriff as he surveyed the carnage. "But why all the shootin'? It looks like just a good old fight to me."

"Oh that's all it was," said Silas sarcastically, "if you don't count one of them trying to gut Luke with a knife, and t'other one trying to backshoot him with a Sharps."

About then, up walked the first Sloniker whose name was Rube. His right ear was puffed out, his nose crushed and swollen, and his eyes were starting to turn colorful shades of red, black, and purple. He was holding what remained of his Sharps rifle in his hands.

"Look here, Sheriff, I just paid twenty-seven-fifty for this here rifle only six months ago. He didn't have any call to do that."

Tom LeBeau looked at the rifle, a smile playing around the corners of his mouth. "Forty yards away, you did this from forty yards away?" He looked at Luke.

Luke said nothing—he considered the question rhetorical.

"Well, Rube, from what people here are telling me,

you intended to use that rifle for some killin' of your own, and shooting someone in the back with a cannon like that sure ain't nice."

Rube sidestepped the observation. "You know how many buffalo I have to kill to pay for that? Why I have to kill six, and skin 'em, and scrape 'em, and stake out the hides. That's after all the rest of us kills six, that's almost a hundred."

"Not quite," observed Tom LeBeau dryly. "Look at it this way, it's not a total loss, you still might be able to use the barrel."

"Uh huh, yeah, thanks, so it ain't all ruined, just most of it."

The other three were regaining consciousness, and helping each other up out of the filth of the street. One of them was coughing and spitting repeatedly. They were all staggering, still dazed, and clearly had no wish for further battle.

One of the not-so-sympathetic onlookers called out, "Hey there, Slonikers, it looks like you all are looking to dig gold right here in the street—with your teeth."

"Yeah," cackled another, "you looked just like a big old shovel, standing straight up, 'cept you were upside down. Hee, hee, hee, hee."

"And," sang out a third, "it was nice of you fellows to donate that nice Sharps for target practice—'cept didn't anyone ever tell you it wasn't supposed to be the target, just the prize? Haw, haw, haw, haw."

The general feeling of mirth and hilarity was lost on the remaining three Slonikers as they groaned, and helped each other up.

Sing Loo retrieved his can of peaches. "Ah good, it's not broken."

"Well, Sheriff, do you have any need of me?" Luke asked.

"No, no, I guess not, I just wish you boys could have settled this without shooting."

"I tried."

"Yes, yes, I guess you did. Staying in town long?"

"Just long enough to finish loading our supplies."

"Good, good, I don't need any more trouble."

"It appears to me—you didn't have any trouble to start with," Henry observed.

"Well yes, you boys know what I mean."

"Yes Sheriff, I'm afraid they do," added Silas, a faint tone of contempt creeping into his voice.

Andrew and Jerome walked down the street and up to Luke. "Could we have a word with you?" Jerome asked.

Luke was brushing some of the dried mud from the back of his trousers and shirt and looked up. "Sure."

"I'm Jerome Puddington, and this is Andrew Lewis. We're with Wells Fargo."

"Howdy, I'm Luke Dawson and this is Henry Bowen and Sing Loo, both good friends of mine. We're all with the Circle D." They shook hands all around.

"They really are good friends of yours," said Andrew. "It's a good thing they were there to watch your back. Those Sloniker boys don't like to play fair at all. It will sure take away their pride, them getting beaten up like that, and they may want revenge."

As if to put an exclamation point on what Andrew just said, Rube Sloniker, his face looking worse by the minute, turned around from helping his kinfolk. He shook what remained of his rifle at Luke, and in doing so the shattered buttstock fell off and landed on the ground with a plop. He bent over to pick up the butt-stock, thinking he might salvage the iron buttplate. The blood rushed to his face, intensifying the pain, and he groaned.

"You ain't seen the last of us," Rube called out gri-macing at the effort.

"I didn't want to see the first of you," Luke sallied back.

The humor was lost on Rube who had nothing more to say. All the Slonikers staggered into the nearest saloon aptly named Trail's End to drink away some of their pain. Another of them, Rafe, had a red crescent in the middle of his forehead in the shape of the rim of a peach can. It appeared to have been branded there.

Turning back to Andrew and Jerome, Luke said, "What can I do for you?"

"First, we'd kind of like to know how old you are, just out of curiosity," said Jerome.

"I'll be 18 in a month, why?"

"No offense, but you can sure fight and shoot for bein' that young," Andrew added.

"Age is relative in how you apply it. In a bottle of whisky, or in a horse, eighteen would be ancient."

Andrew and Jerome looked at Luke, then at each other, then back at Luke.

"Uh huh," said Andrew.

"I wasn't much older when I was riding one hundred miles a shift for Russell, Majors, and Waddell back in '60. What we're looking for is someone who can handle himself and might be available for some special assignments for Wells Fargo. Have you been with the Circle D very long?" Jerome asked.

Henry snorted, Sing Loo chuckled, and Luke just grinned.

"Wha'd I say?" asked Jerome.

"Nothing, nothing at all," said Luke "It's just that my dad owns the Circle D, so you could say that I've been a hand there most of my life."

"So you're Colonel Prentiss Dawson's son," said Andrew.

"You know my dad?"

"Not well, I've driven supplies to him a few times, but he's a fair man, a good man. Now that you tell me you're his son, I can sure see the resemblance between the two of you."

"Being the colonel's son, I don't suppose that you would consider any other type of work than ranching?" Jerome asked.

"That's not necessarily the case at all," Luke said. "However, I'd have to know more about what you're thinking and, of course, talk it over with the colonel. I wouldn't be available for anything until after spring roundup."

"You boys have to get back to the ranch tonight?" Jerome queried.

Luke, Sing Loo, and Henry all looked at each other and then looked back.

"Nope," answered Luke.

"Well then let us put you up at the Dodge House, compliments of Wells Fargo. I can lay out, in a preliminary form, what we're thinking about, and how you might fit in."

"Sounds good to me," said Luke.

"Food and drink too?" Henry asked.

"Food and drink too," said Jerome.

"And wine?" Sing Loo said.

Jerome looked at the little man with the penetrating almond eyes. "And wine," he said.

"Let's do it," said Luke. "We can put the supplies in the store, and run the rig down to the livery stable, then get an early start in the morning."

Luke didn't have an inkling then, but he had just made their trip back to the ranch much more complicated.

Chapter Nine

That night, the Dodge House put on a great spread for the five men. They had all the steak and potatoes they could eat, and enough berry pie to fill them to bursting. Sing Loo got his wine, and Henry had a few drinks of Kentucky bourbon. Luke chose not to drink. Not that he was a teetotaler, he just liked to keep a clear head, something the colonel had impressed on him on more than one occasion.

Dinner was a festive affair, with a few of the townsmen dropping by the table to congratulate Luke, Sing Loo, and Henry for their dealing with the Slonikers. Luke was modest in his acceptance of praise, but inside he felt a small private glow. He could tell from the expressions on Sing Loo and Henry that they felt the same way.

The barber, Floyd Haskins, himself a Civil War veteran, couldn't stop chuckling as he recounted the day's events. "I've seen people crawl out of a fight before, but you actually made that one eat dirt. And, I almost busted a gut laughing when you made that Sharps rifle into a piece of junk. Then old Rube Sloniker shook it at you, and it fell apart in his hands. Ho ho!"

Luke asked, "Do you know them, Floyd?"

"Know 'em well enough to stay clear of 'em. They've never been near my shop, you can tell that just by looking at 'em."

The table chuckled appreciatively.

"You all be careful, you might not have heard the last of them."

"That's the second time I've heard that today," observed Luke.

The Wells Fargo offer, as laid out by Jerome, was fairly simple and straightforward. "What we're thinking about Luke, is to have you, and a very few people like you, as a sort of private investigative and police force for Wells Fargo. This might entail posing as someone you are not or, perhaps, just investigating crimes against Wells Fargo."

"Would I carry a badge?"

"Not in most jurisdictions, however, there is that possibility on occasion. But Wells Fargo would always pay you, regardless of what other income you might generate in your assignment."

"Including rewards on wanted men?"

"Good question! Especially including rewards on wanted men! We want people of any criminal stripe put behind bars, or otherwise disposed of. It will make the whole area safer to settle and that's good for everyone, including Wells Fargo. Although, in order to foster good relations with local law, it's sometimes best to spread the rewards around."

"I have to talk it over with the colonel and won't be able to let you know for a few months. I think I'd really like to do this. Say, I don't want to put you on the spot but what about Henry here? I know he's a great shot!" Luke smiled and clapped Henry on the shoulder.

Henry choked a little on the mouthful he was chewing and looked over at Luke.

Jerome and Andrew exchanged glances, and looked back at Luke and Henry. "To tell you the truth, we talked about Henry and we liked the way he handled himself today. We're convinced he can shoot. It's just that we didn't want to recruit too much from one spread at one time, and we talked to you first, Luke," said Jerome.

Luke understood fully what they were saying now and nodded his head. They wanted him first, but they would hire Henry too.

"Okay if we talk again after roundup?"

"You bet it is," said Andrew. "And whichever way you boys decide, we want to thank you, all of you, for a very entertaining afternoon. I don't know when I've had more fun watching a fracas like that."

"Well, gentlemen thank you very much for the dinner and the accommodations," Luke added. They shook hands all around.

Chapter Ten

They got underway at 9:00 the next morning. Silas didn't open his store until 8:00, and the boys weren't in a hurry to get back to the ranch, so they exchanged pleasantries and leisurely loaded the buckboard. The day appeared to be another pleasant one with the real heat promising to come at mid-afternoon. There were some dark clouds forming on the horizon, but if there was a squall, it would probably pass to the south of them.

They were all dressed in range clothes, even Sing Loo, who had shed his cook's garb. He looked funny, with his queue hanging down behind his Stetson. Henry was riding his paint, letting it go into a gentle trot to keep up with the buckboard. The road along the

Arkansas River was dusty. It had been a long time since any rain had fallen.

All three of them saw it at the same instant in the rocks, a good half-mile away. It was just a faint glint, like a kid playing with a fragment of a mirror. Henry's reaction was one of puzzlement; Sing Loo's one of curiosity. Luke's reaction was one of immediate alarm. It looked like the reflection one might see off a piece of metal—or a rifle barrel.

"Sing, there's a stand of cottonwood trees off to the right about seventy-five yards. I want you to ease over there, as if we are going to rest."

Luke turned around. "Henry, there off to the right, get to the cottonwoods, and go slow unless you hear shooting."

They hadn't gone ten yards when something that sounded like an angry bee whizzed in front of their faces. They looked over and saw puffs of smoke coming from the rocks. Four seconds later they could hear the sound of the big rifles, like claps of thunder, in the distance. Where the other slugs went they never knew. What they did know was that they had to get under cover, and as fast as they could.

"Duck and go," Luke shouted. "Duck and go!"

Henry got as low as he could, and ran his horse to the trees. Luke and Sing Loo crouched over, and whipped the buckboard horses as hard as they could. The buckboard clattered and bounced over the rough ground.

They all made the cover of the trees, but they weren't really safe. The bullets came whining in and around them, with the gun reports following eerily four seconds later.

"What are we going to do?" Henry exclaimed. "These Winchesters don't have anywhere near the range of those big buffalo guns."

"Henry, take your knife and cut me a straight branch about five feet long and get me a strip of rawhide."

"What are you going to do, make a bow and arrow?" Henry asked as another bullet went whizzing by.

"Just do it, Henry, hurry."

Luke took his own knife and cut two of the same size branches. He took Henry's branch and the rawhide strip and bound the three of them together at the top, to form a tripod. "Henry, throw a few rounds at them from your Colts, it might distract them. Sing Loo, bring me a case of .44-40 ammunition."

"Gosh, Luke it would almost make me laugh if I was one of them. Is that what we're going to do, make them die laughing?" Henry obligingly emptied his two Colts in the direction of the rocks. The pistol explosions sounded like the pop of a whip in comparison to the deep booms from far off.

Sing Loo crouched very low, and brought back a case of ammunition. Luke ducked down and retrieved his Winchester from the buckboard. He set the tripod up beside a tree. Then he placed Sing Loo behind the tree.

"Any time I pause in shooting, or if my rifle gets low, I want you to shove shells in the loading gate, okay?"

"Okay, Luke."

"Henry, stand behind that other tree, and tell me if you can see where my bullets are landing, okay?"

"Okay, Luke."

Luke balanced the front of the rifle's loading tube, which was just under the barrel, on the top of the tri-pod. He braced the side of the rifle against the tree, leaving the loading gate open for Sing Loo. Then he tilted the Winchester up at about a twenty-five-degree angle and began firing. He could see from the puffs of dust that he was 200 yards short.

Henry, finally understanding and being very im-pressed, called out, "You're about two hundred yards short, Luke."

Luke adjusted the Winchester to about a thirty-three-degree angle, and fired five more rounds in rapid succession. The rifle sounded like a deeper whip crack, though nothing like the buffalo guns' cannon-like roar. Luke's bullets hit ten yards short of the rocks.

"Ten yards shy, Luke, only ten yards," Henry whooped with glee.

Luke took out his knife, and made a notch in the tree to mark his aiming position, so he could brace the rifle just in front of the receiver. The big buffalo slugs were still coming in, making their angry bee sounds. Two slugs had hit the tree Sing Loo was standing behind.

One slug had taken Henry's hat off when he looked around his tree. The slugs were not coming fast, however, because the powerful buffalo guns were single shot, and the heavy barrels would overheat with rapid firing. Sing Loo was steadily loading shells into Luke's rifle. The loading gate made a click sound as each one went into the loading tube. Luke made a very slight final adjustment and began firing. He worked the lever action on the rifle very fast, and it took on a rhythm of its own. The rifle spit out seventeen pellets of death, all travelling up at the proper angle, and all landing in and around the rocks. The effect was not unlike that of a mortar used in the Civil War.

"Load 'er up Sing," Luke said.

Sing Loo proceeded to reload the rifle very fast. Luke lined up with his firing mark on the tree, and emptied the Winchester again this time using a slower, more controlled rate of fire. Luke repeated this operation five more times, even raising the rifle a slight degree to hit behind the rocks, for a total of 119 rounds. The rapid fire was not unlike that of a Gatling gun, the first practical machine gun of the Civil War, built in 1862. The firing from the rocks ceased. The barrel of Luke's Winchester was hot to the touch. The powder smoke was thick and the smell was sharp in the early spring air.

From the rocks was a silence. It was as if no one had been there.

"Whoa Luke, where did you ever learn something

like that?" Henry inquired. Henry was shaking a little from the released tension.

Sing Loo's eyes were wide, "That was close, Luke. That was too, too close." The back of his shirt was covered with sweat, but he too was slightly shivering.

"I couldn't agree more Sing, one of those Sharps slugs would tear a man apart," Luke said.

Luke and Sing Loo went back to the buckboard, and swung it cautiously out of the cover and onto the road. Henry had retrieved his paint and was riding about thirty yards away, but abreast of them. He was carrying his Winchester across his saddle. They stopped fifty yards away from the rocks. Luke gave Sing Loo his rifle and drew both of his Colts, and they both advanced around the left side of the rocks. Henry ground-hitched his paint and warily scouted around the right side of the rocks, Winchester held at the ready. The sun was high overhead, bringing down a welcoming midday heat to the three tense men. Insects were making noise, and a bird had started to chirp. Overhead, a hawk was floating, circling lazily in the sky, waiting for an unwary animal to come out of its burrow.

The three converged at the back of the rocks, where they saw two blood trails on the ground. The rocks had several little marks on them, as if they'd been lightly hit with a miner's pickaxe. It also looked as though there could have been several ricochets. One blood trail was considerably larger than the other. The blood trails blended with horse tracks, and faded off into the distance. They also found a canteen, with a bullet hole through it and some blood on one side, along with many long, empty cartridge casings of .50 caliber. There were also four empty bottles of whiskey, the half-gallon variety, and a half-chewed plug of tobacco. Up in the rocks, they found a dead body, staring sightlessly up at the sky. In the middle of his forehead, along with a bullet hole, was a big red crescent-shaped welt.

"Well boys, I'd say old Rafe Sloniker has skinned his last buffalo," Henry said.

"I did not know him, but I did not like him," said Sing Loo.

"Well Sing, I'd say the impression you made on him was a lasting one," Luke dryly observed. "We were real lucky we dawdled a little bit in town."

"How's that, Luke?" asked Henry.

"Well, first we gave these old boys a lot of time to drink up all that John Barleycorn they brought with them and, because of that, their aim wasn't any good. Then, if we hadn't come along at just the right time to see their gun barrels in the sun, we'd have been done for. It wouldn't have mattered how drunk they were. If we'd gotten within two hundred yards of them, there would have been no way for them to miss with those big buffalo rifles."

"What should we do with him, Luke?" said Henry, indicating Rafe.

"Let's take him down to the riverbank and cave an overhang in on him, though it's more than he deserves. Henry, would you ride back and get the tripod? We'll leave it there, in case any of them come back. They'll know where he is. Although, the way they hightailed it, I doubt we'll see any of 'em any time soon. They must have been in a real hurry, they left a half bottle of whiskey up in the rocks."

"What if we took him back to town?"

Luke looked steadily at Henry for a moment, "And talk to Tom LeBeau? You met him. What do you think?"

Henry mulled it over and then gave a laugh. "He'd say it was out of his jurisdiction and nothing to do with him."

"That's exactly what he'd say." Luke chuckled. "Well, let's get to it."

So they went to work quickly because Rafe didn't smell any better now than when he was alive; worse, if that was possible. They found a hollowed-out part of ground by the river, and rolled him in and collapsed the ground on him. Henry retrieved the tripod, and they set it up by the riverbank where they'd planted Rafe.

The three started off again. Henry still stayed thirty yards away. About ten miles on they decided to take a break, and stopped by another group of trees.

"Luke, how did you ever think of tying those sticks together, and bracing that Winchester to shoot at them? I'd have been shot to doll rags before I thought of anything like that."

"Yes Luke, how did you do that? That was very clever," Sing Loo added.

"I can't take much credit for it. The Indians have been shooting arrows up in the air to come down from a high angle since the white men built the first fort in this country, and probably a long time before that. The colonel and I have fired pistols at three hundred yards."

"Three hundred yards? Pistols? How!" exclaimed Henry.

"Much the same way as we did here, by lying down and bracing the pistol, and walking the shots in to the target. Of course, it only works if there's a dry spell so you can see the puffs of dust where your bullet is hitting. Oh, and you have to be on fairly level ground for the same reason. I never had tried it with a rifle before, but I thought it might work."

"Lord, were we lucky," said Henry.

"I think the Lord had a lot to do with it, because there were a lot of things that had to happen for us to survive. As foul and crude as the Slonikers are, they know how to set up an ambush. It's how they make a living. They do the same thing they did here when they set up to shoot buffalo, or any other living thing."

The trio didn't talk much the rest of the trip back. They were keeping a wary eye on anything that might provide cover for an ambush. They watched trees, rocks, high ground, and even scoured the area for any freshly dug holes, but found nothing suspicious.

As they pulled up to the main house, Pete came out the door. His scar was a bright red, and his eyes a deep green.

Before Pete could say a word, Luke asked, "What's wrong, Pete?"

"Ain't no way to sugarcoat it, Luke, your pa's been shot."

Chapter Eleven

Luke threw the reins aside, and stood up. "How bad?"

"Through the shoulder, and a graze on the head, but if the colonel hadn't been falling they would have killed him. They shot him in the back, the cowards, and they killed Fury too."

Fury, one of the new hands, was a young man with as high a spirit as his nickname indicated. In spite of the name, he loved jokes. He would never play another joke.

Luke was quick out of the buckboard, but Sing Loo was quicker, as he raced into the house, "I am going to look," he said.

Henry hung back to talk to Pete. "What happened?"

"That new rancher, Richard Hawthorne, decided to cut himself a wide swath. He's laying claim to about ten thousand acres of federal land and about two thousand acres of the Circle D."

"How did he figure to get away with that?"

"There's no law out here, but most folk are pretty decent. The colonel will even give a beef or two to folks down on their luck or to Indians passing through."

"Luke said you have never had any Indian trouble."

"Never have. Now this buffoon thinks he can just sashay in, and take the land. He set it up real cute too."

"What'd he do?"

"He started putting up some of that bob-wire fence on Circle D land. Fury and the colonel were just out riding. The colonel was showing him Circle D territory when they spotted the work crew, and rode over to talk. Two men were working and three were just standing around. That should have been a warning."

"Yeah, then what happened?"

"The colonel asked what they were doing. George Sly, this fast gun, said, 'What's it look like? Fencing off Bar H land, what are you going to do about it?' "

"The work crew had stopped, and gotten out of the way. They went over to the wagon to get their weapons. The other two men faded, five yards off to each side. The colonel had figured out the set up and told Fury, 'Let's go, it's a stacked deck.' About that time George Sly said, 'I always heard Circle D boys were yellow, starting with the owner. This is going to be easier than I thought.' Before the colonel could stop him, Fury was turning his horse around. At that point it wouldn't have mattered what they did. George Sly shot Fury in the side of the head and the colonel in the shoulder. Luckily, someone else grazed his head on the way down."

"Luckily?"

"Yeah, luckily. First, because it was a graze and then, because it bled like a stuck hog. There was so much blood, they thought for sure the colonel was dead too, so they didn't pump any more bullets into him. Although he was wounded and dazed, he heard them all laughing and bragging about how it was the easiest hundred they'd ever made. I guess George got five hundred dollars for having set it up. We went out and found them eight hours later. The colonel was more dead than alive."

Luke walked into his dad's room, where Sing was already gently removing the bandages to inspect the wounds. Prentiss was slightly propped up in bed. His skin was the color of the belly of a day-old fish. The colonel looked up, and said in a weak whisper, "It's not as bad as it looks, Luke. I've had falls off of horses that were worse than this." Somehow Luke doubted that.

Sing Loo looked up at Luke. "I need boiling water, which I will have Maria get. I need to make poultice."

"You look fine, Dad," Luke lied. "You just need to get some rest for a few days, and you'll be all right."

Luke found it very hard to hide the pain he was feeling. The memory of his mother lying dead in his arms burned like a fire in him. Now here was his father almost murdered in a similar fashion.

"Luke, you look worse than I feel," the colonel whispered, trying to cheer Luke up. "Look at it this way, they picked a bad time to try this. We've got a full complement of twenty-five hands, including many good fighters and all of them mad." The colonel closed his eyes, exhausted at the effort of speaking.

Sing Loo bustled in carrying a pan of hot water and a pile of clean cloths. He put these down on the table and bustled back out. Pretty soon back he came with another pan of liquid, this one giving off a noxious odor.

"Whew Sing, is that the remains of those eggs you buried a few years ago?" asked Luke.

Sing Loo chuckled. He went to work with a purpose. Luke marveled at how gentle Sing's touch was. After carefully bathing the wounds, Sing Loo prepared the poultice. He applied the poultice to the entrance and exit wounds of the shoulder and the scalp wound. They were already turning an angry red. After binding the wounds, Sing hurried back out. Sing came back carrying a glass with a light brown clear liquid.

"Here, Colonel sir, drink. You need to sleep one or two days."

"I doubt that, Sing," the colonel wheezed, "I haven't been able to sleep more than an hour at a time since this happened."

"I know, please drink."

The colonel did as he was asked. In fact he did feel terrible, and the wound had started to hurt much more, not less. His face was red and feverish. Luke got up, and gave his dad a very rare kiss on the head, and walked softly out the room. With a monumental effort, he fought back the tears of grief and rage.

Dusk had settled in, and the day was swiftly moving toward night. Luke walked out to the front stoop. Pete and Henry were still there, talking in low tones. "Pete, come on in. You too, Henry, there's a lot to talk about."

"I'm sorry Luke, we would have sent someone in last night if we'd known you were going to stay in Dodge."

"We were delayed a little bit."

Pete glanced at Henry's Stetson with the hole through it. "So I gathered."

Luke lit the coal oil lamps. They sat down on the overstuffed furniture, the odor of horsehair very slight in the air. Maria brought in some fresh baked tortillas, and a plate piled high with well-done strips of beef. Sing Loo brought coffee, then crept noiselessly down the hall to check on the colonel. He came back a few moments later. "He is sleeping."

"Thanks, Sing," said Luke. "Thanks a lot."

They ate in silence, each alone with their own thoughts. Finally Luke said, "Pete, I want you to think about what I am going to say. I believe the Circle D has to go on a war footing. Dick Hawthorne is not going to rest until we are driven out of the country, don't you agree with me?"

"That's the way it appears to me, Luke. I almost rode out looking for George and Dick, just after we found Fury and the colonel. When we saw the colonel was still alive though, I thought getting him back to the ranch was most important."

"I'm sure glad you got my dad back here, and didn't go looking for them, they'd have been waiting for you. Who is this George Sly anyway?"

"A real tough talker, supposed to have killed three Mexicans south of the border and four cowboys in Dallas last fall. He puts notches on his guns. A real sidewinder."

"You ever hear of him, Henry?" Luke asked.

Henry nodded. "Yeah, he likes to prove how fast he is on people he's sure he can beat. I guess he might have killed a couple of Texans, but I don't know if they were sober though."

"Okay, first thing tomorrow, I want to meet all the hands here. We'll double their wages until this whole thing is over, they'll earn it. If anyone doesn't want to stay he can be paid off with no hard feelings. Right now, we want only men who can fight. They'll eat in shifts, and patrol only in groups of four—spread out. Their shifts will be fifteen to eighteen hours a day, not the usual twelve. One more thing—George Sly is mine."

"Now, wait a minute, Luke," Pete interjected.

"No, I mean it Pete. I have to be the bait. They think the colonel is dead, and I'm the only obstacle to their getting the Circle D. I have to draw them out or they'll just sneak around. I'll want backup, but I want George Sly." Luke sat on the edge of his chair. His blue eyes had turned slate gray, and his face was hard, harder than anyone had ever seen.

Pete looked over at Henry. "Are you ready for all this Henry? It really isn't your fight."

Henry merely nodded, but Luke said, "Henry saved my bacon in Dodge, and was a big help on the way back. If it weren't for Henry, Pete, I wouldn't be sitting here now."

Pete stood up. "That's good enough for me, what do you say we get some sleep? We've got a big day tomorrow."

Luke and Henry stood up also. "Sounds good, I'll see you tomorrow. Oh, Pete, would you get Henry settled in at the bunkhouse?"

"Sure thing, Luke, and if you hear anyone moving around tonight it will probably be one of the boys. I'm putting five on watch."

"Good thinking, thanks. See you in the morning."

Luke tiptoed down the hall to check on his dad. Sing Loo was in the room. He saw Luke and came out.

"The colonel is sleeping. He will sleep for one or two days then feel better."

"I can't thank you enough, Sing."

Sing Loo nodded, half bowed, then went back in the colonel's room. Luke got down on his knees, and prayed for his dad's recovery. The night passed slowly. Luke tossed and turned, but sleep eluded him until almost dawn.

Chapter Twelve

At the meeting next morning, Pete and Luke laid out the rules for the men. They all had grim expressions. A few had wry grins at the mention of double wages, wondering if they would live to spend them. Only one man, Jack McGaw, came up to Pete after the meeting. "I'm sorry, Pete, but I have to draw my time. I was in one of these range wars back in Texas in '69, and I swore I'd never get in another one."

Pete gave him a cold look. "Best we find out now who can be counted on, and who can't."

"Now, Pete, you said you wouldn't have any hard feelings."

"Luke said he wouldn't. Here, here's what you've got coming, take it and ride out—now." Pete counted out some specie into Jack's hand. Jack knew that for as long as Pete was there, he should not come back to the Circle D. The rest of the hands avoided looking at Mc-Gaw as he made his way back to the bunkhouse to get his gear.

Luke walked up to Pete. "Just the one man leaving?"

"Yep, good riddance."

Luke gave a sad smile, and shook his head.

"What do you want to do first, Luke?"

"Let's go back to where they ambushed Dad and Fury. We can take some tools and start to pull some fence. What do you think?"

Pete nodded his head. "That should open the ball."

"Even though every man doesn't own a rifle, let's make sure he has one to carry now."

"Yeah," Pete said, "I know we have plenty of the Model 66s and they've most all been converted from rim-fire to center-fire. The hands don't typically carry a rifle when they're out on the ranch, as you know, what with the rope and all, it can give the horses blisters. Since they will still have work to do, I'm going to have them mount the rifles at the rear of their saddles."

"Good idea, Pete. We'll need all the firepower we can get."

"How do you want to do this?"

"I figured I'd take Rowdy, Tex, and Henry for backup."

"And me," said Pete.

"Aw Pete, there's a lot that has to be looked after here. Who are we going to leave?"

"You forgot about Mike, he's plenty steady and has been at the Circle D for four years. Besides I'm just goin'."

"You're right, Mike's a good man. I just hoped you'd stay here that's all."

"Think I'm too old?"

"No."

"Too slow?'

"Too ornery maybe. No, Pete, it's just that you're Dad's best friend."

"And you're his son. Think I'd be anywhere else?"

"Okay, I give up. Thanks Pete."

Luke wasn't surprised to see Rowdy and Tex ride up and demand to go along. He considered them more like close friends than ranch hands.

Rowdy Applegate was only five and a half feet tall but he weighed over 180 pounds with no fat. His blond hair contrasted with his deep blue eyes that crinkled when he smiled, which was often. He wore a Stetson hat, checkered flannel shirt, canvas riding pants, and custom high brown boots. He'd been with the colonel for five years.

Tex Slocum was Rowdy's partner. Since he was from Arkansas, no one knew how he got the name Tex but him. Tex was a six-footer, and weighed about the same as Rowdy. They also dressed similarly with Tex preferring custom low cut boots, but with high leather leggings. Tex had brown hair, brown eyes, and an expression like a hound dog. If he didn't have to talk at all, Tex would be happy. When he did speak it was usually with a laconic "yep" or "nope" in answer to a question. He and Rowdy had just ridden in to the Circle D one day five years ago, and never left.

As they rode out Luke was thinking, *What do I know about this man George Sly I'm going to face? He's probably fast. He's a killer. He'll take any kind of advantage he can in a fight. He likes to rattle people with rough talk, and force their hand, so he can draw first. I'm going to have to rattle him, to get him off balance. What about Dick Hawthorne? Will he be there? What do I do about him if he is?*

They rode farther out. Luke observed that the grass was good, both the stem grass and the buffalo grass farther up. He knew that the cattle preferred the sweet buffalo grass. In fact Luke had seen this preference in action on many occasions when they would dig down through the snow to get at it in winter, rather than eat the hay that was provided for them by the Circle D. Sometimes the cattle would play with the hay and spread it around, but would seldom eat it if they could get to the buffalo grass.

The sun was shining brightly in the new morning sky. It was another beautiful day. *A good day, as good as any to die,* thought Luke.

Henry rode up and said, "Luke, since I've met you

I've seen more action than in the past seven years—total." Luke chuckled.

They rode first to the spot where Fury was murdered, and the colonel badly wounded. The Bar H fence crew was about a quarter mile away, still working on putting up the barbed wire. The Circle D hands rode up, spread out ten yards apart, and Luke was in the middle. They reined their horses in about thirty yards away and, as if on signal, all dismounted. Everyone, except Luke, grabbed their rifles out of the scabbards. They all advanced, still at ten yard intervals. The buffalo grass swished as they walked through it.

When they first sighted the Circle D riders, the Bar H work crew scrambled into their wagon and retrieved their weapons. They were a relaxed bunch because they knew how fast George Sly was. He'd proved it on several occasions.

Luke saw that they looked confident and were probably looking forward to those big bonuses. There were seven of them, including George Sly, with only two making any pretense that they were working. Luke flicked the thongs off the hammers of his pistols as he walked up. They all stopped ten yards away.

George Sly was full of himself. He looked like he'd read too many dime novels. If the situation hadn't been so deadly, Luke could have almost laughed. Sly was about five and a half feet tall and weighed maybe 140 pounds. To compensate for his small stature, he wore a high-crowned black Stetson hat, and custom black high-heeled boots. In addition, he wore black buck cord pants and a black leather two-gun rig, carried low and tied down. His Colts had white one-piece ivory grips, and he wore a gleaming white gambler's shirt. Luke immediately saw how the blending of shirt and grips were meant to confuse an unwary opponent. Sly's pinched face and cruel black eyes were overshadowed by a huge handlebar mustache. His pallid skin indicated he'd spent little time in the sun. The softness of his hands showed no familiarity with ranch work, but much time with cards—and guns.

Sly spotted Luke right off, as Luke looked like a younger version of his father. "Well, well, it looks like the cub is gonna try what the he-wolf couldn't do."

"You're Sly?"

"That's right and you've just made the biggest mistake of your life you little—"

"Shut up, Sly, I've heard about you," Luke exclaimed, throwing Sly off balance.

Sly wasn't used to being interrupted. When he was working himself up to a gunfight, most people were intimidated. "You've heard what?" he sneered.

"I've heard that you're a slimy little backshooting coward, who never meets men straight on. This ought to be something new for you." This latter part wasn't entirely accurate, but Luke thought he'd air his suspicions. Luke stood there, appearing calm, arms crossed left over right. His hands rested just over the butts of his pistols.

Sly started laughing a mean, menacing little laugh, which sounded like the rattle of a snake. He reached up with his left hand to take his Stetson off, in an attempt at deflecting Luke's attention, as if to let out more of the laugh. Simultaneously, he dropped his right hand to his pistol to draw it. The effort was wasted.

With blazing speed, Luke drew his Colt and cocked it. No one could have timed the hesitation as Luke lined up on the third button of Sly's white shirt. The explosion of Luke's Colt and the crimson flower on Sly's shirt happened at the same instant. Luke's slug drove the pearl button through Sly's stomach and out his back.

George Sly was supposed to be fast. His gun didn't even make it halfway out of the holster. Sly dropped his hat and grabbed his stomach, pain etched in every fiber of his being. All he could say was, "Oh—oh—oh."

Luke looked at him without pity; his only feeling was that of contempt. "Does it hurt, Sly? Bet it does. Well Fury doesn't feel anything, and the 'he-wolf' isn't feeling any too good either. They're both better men than you are, and a hundred like you. Here, this will make you feel better."

With that, Luke shot him through the mouth. The lower left side of his mustache was also taken off which gave Sly a comical, uneven, final appearance. Sly went over on his back, his eyes unseeing, his right hand still on his pistol. Luke's stomach roiled only a little at this event. Close up though it was, he knew there was no other way and what he did was right. He took no pleasure in the killing. However, Luke did judge it to be necessary, like shooting a rabid dog.

The Circlc D hands leveled their rifles on the horrified Bar H men. Pete Ryan was actually chuckling. "I guess now when we call somebody empty headed we can just call them, 'Sly-headed.' "

Luke reloaded, then whipped his pistol back in the holster, and dropped his arms to his sides. "Which of you men were here the day before yesterday?"

Two of the Bar H men immediately backed up, their hands held high in the air. The Circle D men had moved in. "Hold it," said Henry.

"We weren't here, this ain't got nothin' to with us," one of them whined.

"You were ready to jump right in, if the fight had gone the other way," Rowdy growled.

Luke addressed the four men left. "Which one of you brave men did the shooting?"

Two more men quickly backed away with their hands held high. "We was just on the work crew, we didn't shoot at nobody," one of them said.

"Yeah, right," said Tex. For Tex, this was speaking volumes. The Circle D hands all looked at Tex then back at the Bar H.

Of the two remaining, one more backed away, his hands held high. "I didn't do no shootin', that was George Sly there and Zeb here." He indicated Sly on the ground and the one left, Zeb, by pointing with his chin. He still held his hands high in the air.

Luke turned his attention to the remaining man, "Zeb, huh? You quite a backshooter, Zeb?"

The man named Zeb just stood there. His skin had turned a sickly pale color under his Kansas tan. "I didn't do—I didn't mean—I mean—I—I."

"Yeah, I know what you mean, you're real sorry— that you got caught. You're wearing iron, pull it!"

Zeb dropped to his knees. He held his arms out in front of him in supplication. His brown eyes were wide in terror. His pistol, a Colt, was worn high on his hip for convenience in carrying, not drawing. Clearly, he was no threat as a fast gun, nor was he seeking a reputation as one. "Please mister, I know I did wrong. On my best day I couldn't have come close to pulling iron with George Sly. I-I promise if you let me out of this, you'll never see me again."

Luke looked over at the other five men. "Any of you want to take his place? Maybe I ought to turn around since you seem to like to shoot at a man's back." The other five all seemed to find something real interesting on the ground about five feet in front of them. Their hands were held high in the air, and raised higher still after Luke's challenge.

"All right, all of you put your weapons in the wagon. Put Sly's in there too. He won't be needing them anymore. Take out the fence tools and bring them over here. You, Zeb, use your hat, and take every cent you boys have and put it in. Start with the five hundred in blood money from Sly and the hundred each from you scum. If I find one cent held back or 'forgotten' I'll shoot off a finger."

"Tie your horses to the back of the wagon," said Pete. Luke looked at him and nodded.

The Bar H hands, realizing they might live to tell of this day, were quick to comply with every demand.

"Anybody got anything in their boots?" Zeb asked. "I ain't aiming to lose a finger 'cause somebody got greedy." Two of them sat down, and began shaking out their boots. Some folded bills fell out. Rowdy scowled.

"Can I search them now, Luke?"

"Go ahead, Rowdy."

Rowdy took out his razor-sharp Bowie knife, and advanced on the hapless and by now thoroughly cowed men. He proceeded to slice the pockets off of every one of their pants and shirts. He wasn't gentle or neat. There were a few nicks here and there accompanied by a muffled curse, or a howl. Rowdy walked back with a smile of distinct pleasure. "I guess they were honest for once in their sorry lives, Luke. I didn't find anything else on them."

"It's a good thing, or they would have been missing some fingers." All the Bar H crew looked at each other, then back at Luke. They were a miserable sight with their clothes hanging in tatters and a few drops of blood scattered about.

"I know you'll be happy to learn that your money is a donation to Fury's next of kin. Fury's the one that you scum murdered." They didn't seem all that happy. "Now pick up those tools and start removing that fence. Two of you cut it, and the other four dig out posts. Move!"

Luke knew that generally it was much easier to tear something down than it was to build it up and so it was with the fence. Being highly motivated with threats, curses, and an occasional punch, the Bar H crew tore down almost all of what had been built up over the previous week in just a few hours. Pete made them stack the posts in a pile and in no time there was a huge fire going.

Towards the late afternoon, Pete called them all together. The Bar H shrank away from his massive frame as he walked among them. Spying Zeb, Pete unleashed a powerful right hook. It made a splat as it connected with his left cheek and eye. Zeb went down, like a sack of potatoes that had been kicked, with a groan. The third gunman, from the day before yesterday, looked up in terror as Pete advanced on him. A straight right hand from Pete broke his nose with a crunch, and he too went down. The two workmen from the previous time tried to turn away, but Pete grabbed each of their chins in his two large hands. The sound of their heads, as they slammed together, was like that of two stones hitting. These two joined their companions in uneasy slumber. Pete simply glared at the final two as they shrank back, trembling.

"Go haul some water," Pete ordered.

The two still upright Bar H men were quick to obey. They grabbed buckets, ran to the nearest creek, and brought them back full.

"Pour it on them," said Pete indicating the prostrate forms. They did. Two of the men staggered upright, shaking off the water, while the other two were still lying in sweet repose.

"Do it again," growled Pete and the process was repeated. The four of them finally got unsteadily to their feet looking ragged, confused, bleary-eyed, and wet. The pile of posts was crackling merrily.

Luke walked up. "We probably should have shot the bunch of you right off, but we didn't. If I see any of you anywhere again, I'll kill you."

"You mean on this range?" one of them asked.

"I mean anywhere in Kansas, get out!"

"Four of you pick up Sly, and take him with you. You're on Circle D land," said Henry.

"Can we have the wagon at least?" one of them asked, hopefully.

"You get nothin'," growled Rowdy. "You're lucky if we let you keep your boots."

"Yep," said Tex.

Zeb looked at Luke, hesitated, then walked over. The

whole left side of his face looked like an over ripe plum. "When I was on my knees, I don't mind telling you, I was scared, and begging for my life, and you had every right in the world to shoot me . . . But after your pa got shot, I knew he was still alive, and I didn't say nothin'. Well, thanks for sparing me. You ain't going to see me again."

Luke looked at Zeb, and said nothing. Four of them picked up Sly, who looked smaller in death even than he had in life, and started off, followed by Zeb and one other.

Over the crest of a low rise about half a mile away came three riders. The big man in the center was Dick Hawthorne. He stood out because of his distinctive white, sombrero-style, Stetson custom-made hat. They reined up when they saw the fence destruction and the fire. Then one of them spotted the bedraggled procession, and pointed.

Pete's big voice boomed out. "Come on in, Hawthorne, if you got the guts." There was no indication that the three had any intention of accepting Pete's invitation.

Luke went over to his horse and unlimbered his Winchester. "Try to imagine a spot about ten feet above their heads and let's make some noise." And they did. All five of them emptied their rifles at that spot above the three riders. The rifles made a loud repetitive crackling sound, like a long string of firecrackers on the

Fourth of July. Some of the bullets actually sang in uncomfortably close to the riders. One horse got burned on the side and reared up, almost throwing its rider. The trio whirled and rode off. The Bar H procession cringed at the shooting, but with their burden, trudged onward disconsolately. The sweet smell of gunsmoke hung in the dry late afternoon air.

Luke, Henry, Rowdy, and Tex each led a horse while riding their own back to the Circle D. The rest of the horses were tied to the wagon driven by Pete. They had over $1,100 to send to Fury's next of kin, which was certainly not a replacement for the young man, but it still amounted to over three years' normal wages. In a buckskin scabbard was a Sharps .50 caliber buffalo rifle that Luke laid claim to. He also claimed Sly's pistols, and no one gave him any argument on either score. The rest of the boys were offered their pick of the remaining weapons and horses.

"I think the Circle D will buy whatever weapons and horses we don't want from us; the ranch may need to stock up," Pete said.

Luke agreed. "I'm sure that's right, Pete. We can always use horses and we are going to need a lot more weapons." Then Luke chuckled. "Henry and I have been on the wrong end of those big buffalo rifles. I figured we needed one in self-defense for the next trip to Dodge City."

"Amen to that," Henry said as he rode up alongside

Luke. "I've been wondering though, Luke, I mean they're pretty and everything but why did you want Sly's pistols?"

"As a reminder."

"A reminder—of what?"

"If I ever get too full of myself, thinkin' how good I am, or might be, all I have to do is look at the pistols on the wall and remember how good George Sly thought he was."

Chapter Thirteen

When they got back, the first thing they did was to check on the colonel. Luke went inside, and Sing Loo met him at the door.

"The colonel is still asleep."

"Still? Has he been resting easy?"

"He is very comfortable, and breathing well."

"Thanks Sing. When do you think he will be able to talk?"

"Maybe one, maybe two days."

"One or two days? He wasn't sleeping at all before. Sing, what kind of 'who hit John' did you give him?"

"An old Chinese remedy."

"All right, but Sing, he will wake up won't he?" Luke said, only half kidding.

Sing Loo chuckled. "Heh, I will fix him."

"Okay, thanks Sing, thanks for everything."

Luke went out to get Pete, Rowdy, Tex, Mike, and Henry together for a council of war. The hands had all heard of Luke's showdown with George Sly, and they looked at Luke with increased respect, as a man in his own right. They also looked admiringly at the twin Colts of Sly's, and felt there was a little vengeance collected for Fury and the colonel.

"They're going to have to hit us hard someplace," said Pete. "Their confidence is going to be shaken after looking at Sly."

"I'll bet at least half of those boys we sent packing have kept on going," opined Rowdy.

"All of them more likely," quipped Henry.

"Okay," said Luke. "Where are they going to hit us, and how do we react?"

"Well," said Pete. "Here's the way I see it." And they came up with a plan, not just one, but a whole series of plans and contingencies. They mapped out a campaign not unlike one in the Civil War. Luke contributed little to it until the final part of the campaign, and then the plan was all his.

"Where did you come up with that, Luke? Is that one of those Roman things you always read about?" asked Pete.

"No, it's about three thousand years before that in the *Bible*, the Book of Joshua, the eighth chapter," said Luke. "You can find it in later histories too, of course. The Indians did it to Captain Fetterman back in December of '66. It didn't work the first time so they did it again, then it worked real well."

"Much to Fetterman's grief," added Henry.

"That's right, his and eighty others. We'll just give it another twist or two."

Things were quiet around the Circle D for a few days. The hands all carried rifles in addition to their handguns, which they had always carried. Pete still put a night guard around the sleeping areas, and posted others about four hundred yards out. The colonel was awake some and took some nourishment. Still he could only take a few unsteady steps at a time. Even so, that didn't prevent him from wanting to keep a hand in some aspects of planning for the coming conflict.

The following afternoon, Dick Hawthorne and eight riders from the Bar H rode into the main yard of the Circle D. "I want to see Luke Dawson," he said without preamble. Hawthorne was a big man, over six feet tall, and he dressed in the manner of many ranchers. He wore a red pullover muslin shirt with a bibbed front, black buck cord pants, and high custom boots, with a big wide custom white Stetson hat. On his right hip he carried a Colt pistol, butt forward like a lot of former Army men. His face was a florid red, as were his ears, from over exposure to the sun. His eyes were a clear blue. Overall he was a handsome man, and he knew it.

Luke walked out the front door and down the steps. His Colts were unthonged. "I'm Luke Dawson."

"I'm Dick Hawthorne—and I want to talk about buying the Circle D."

"Why? What makes you think it's for sale?"

"Well, I just thought with your pa gone in that unfortunate incident that you might be of a mind to sell. I'll pay good money." He started to dismount.

"Just stay on your horse. You've got a few things wrong, Hawthorne."

"Like what?" Hawthorne said, as he put his right foot back in the stirrup.

"My dad isn't gone. He's still very much alive."

"What?"

"That's right, and that 'unfortunate incident' you refer to was nothing but a bushwacking, murder I call it. As to your 'good money,' I call that blood money. We saw some of it that we took away from that sorry bunch that you sent out to try your same filthy trick two days in a row. We'd sooner give the land back to the Indians, than sell to the likes of you"

"Well George Sly told me—"

"Last time I saw George, he wasn't in any shape to talk. Didn't that bunch you sent out tell you anything?"

"Not much. They left George, I paid them off, and they left."

"Told you," sang out Henry from across the yard. Ten of the Circle D hands had formed a large loose semicircle around the Bar H crowd, their rifles casually resting in the crooks of their arms.

Pete strode up. "You heard what he said, Hawthorne,

Circle D isn't for sale, especially not to you. Now ride on out."

Another rider came up alongside Hawthorne, John Fowler. Fowler was a big man, like his boss, but the similarity ended there. Fowler wore old frontier riding pants, a faded blue flannel shirt, and high custom boots. He had the usual Stetson hat, and was carrying a Smith and Wesson .44 caliber in a cross draw holster. His brown hair was cut short, underneath which he had dark blue eyes, with scar tissue around them both. The nose on his face was flat, and slightly bent off to one side. Handsome, he was not. "I'm John Fowler, of the Bar H."

"I wouldn't be too proud of that," Luke said, "it looks like it's been hard on you."

The Circle D hands openly laughed while a couple of the newer Bar H hands had to turn their heads to hide a smile. Sing Loo had come out on the porch, with a shotgun that was almost as big as he was. His eyes crinkled when he heard Luke's quip. Fowler's eyes widened, then narrowed dangerously.

"You're a real smart one, ain't you?" Fowler said. He looked over at Pete. "You the one that got Sly?" Pete shook his head.

"I shot him," said Luke, "in a place you boys don't usually shoot at, in the front. He was so slow, I could have read a book in the time it took him to get his guns out. You want to see them? I've got them tacked on the wall." The Circle D hands snickered, and the Bar H hands looked glum. They'd seen George Sly shoot plenty of times, and he had been fast.

Pete knew it wasn't like Luke at all to be goading someone like this, not even someone like Fowler. He waited to see what would happen next.

"Maybe you need to be taught a lesson," said Fowler.

Luke looked over at Hawthorne. "Is this what you do, Hawthorne, hire men to do your fighting for you because you're too much of a coward to do it yourself?" Hawthorne gave Luke a hard look but said nothing.

Luke looked back at Fowler. "What kind of a 'lesson' do you have in mind, the same kind as Sly? I don't think you're good enough, but if you do, let's open the ball." Luke backed up a couple of steps. His eyes were a deadly steel blue. He crossed his hands, left over right, and waited. Luke was pushing hard, letting Hawthorne, and the Bar H, know that there was no give here.

Fowler was very quick to unbuckle his pistol. He didn't want anyone, especially Luke, to mistake his intention of definitely not drawing. He dismounted and put his gunbelt around the saddlehorn, "I figure we'll just have us a no-holds-barred fight. That might take some of the starch out of you."

Luke unbuckled his gunrig and handed it to Pete. "You know Fowler, I hear you talking, but I see Hawthorne's hand on the strings over you like a puppet. It must get downright uncomfortable."

The Circle D hands gave a nervous laugh. They were a little worried what might happen with this bigger, and clearly more experienced fighter. The Bar H hands looked forward eagerly to this latest development. Henry walked over to Sing Loo and they stood together. They both had small half-smiles on their faces.

Luke said, "Hey, Hawthorne, when I get through with your puppet here, you and I are going to fight unless you're too yellow."

Hawthorne's face turned a deeper red, but all he could muster up was, "We'll see about that. We'll see what you feel like, after John gets through with you."

The afternoon had darkened. Swirling clouds had formed on the horizon, and a breeze was starting to blow. It looked as if they were going to get some badly needed rain. Fowler also put his hat on his saddlehorn, and turned around. Luke sailed his hat over to Henry. Since they always wore hats in the sun, both combatants now looked like someone had drawn a white ring around the top of their head.

Fowler advanced in a crouch. His scarred fists were held up high, palms in, the current boxing style. Luke was very grateful for Sing Loo's training, and that he did not have to meet Fowler on Fowler's terms. They warily circled each other. Fowler confidently made a couple of short left jabs in the air, then a short right, testing Luke's reactions. Luke easily moved out of harm's way. Luke stood with his right side to Fowler. He held his right arm in a V in front with his left fist held closely behind, a curious position for someone right handed. Fowler moved in, firing a couple of hard lefts and then a long right at Luke, but Luke wasn't there. Luke pivoted, and whirled around to his left. He held out his right arm like a club. At the last instant he whipped the back of his closed fist into Fowler's jaw. Fowler reeled from the impact. A small cut opened up on his cheekbone.

The Circle D hands cheered at this drawing of first blood. "Way to go, Luke," called out Rowdy.

Fowler moved back in, stung, but not really hurt. Luke, still standing with his right side to Fowler, kicked downward at Fowler's shin with the side of his right foot. Fowler reached down to grab Luke's leg, at which point Luke drew it back, and with a high snap kick connected with the side of Fowler's head. Fowler went down. He was hurt, head ringing and throbbing. He was slow to get up.

The Circle D hands were cheering loudly with cries of "Yee haw," and "That's our Luke." The Bar H hands were pensive, and silent.

Fowler moved back in. This time he threw a couple more lefts, then he shifted his weight to his left foot. He swung through with his right foot for a hard kick at Luke's groin. Luke crossed his arms, right over left, low and in front of himself, and blocked the kick, but he didn't let Fowler's leg go. With his right hand he grabbed Fowler's heel, and with his left hand he grabbed the toe. He then twisted them 180 degrees. Fowler had two choices: he could either turn around, awkwardly balanced on one foot, or he could have his knee torn out. He chose to turn around. Luke lifted Fowler's leg up high and stepped in, then used his right foot to sweep Fowler's left leg out from under him. Fowler went face down on the ground with a crash. Fowler got up, slower this time. Luke stepped in and grabbed him by the shirtfront with his left hand. Fowler tried to break the hold, but was too late. Luke used the edge of his right hand, and chopped Fowler twice on the neck just under the jaw. Fowler's eyes rolled back in his head, and he collapsed. He lay there in a heap, unable to get up, or even move. The Bar H hands sat there in stunned silence.

Sing Loo rubbed his hands together and said, "Ah, good."

The Circle D hands went wild with cheering. Luke looked over at Hawthorne. "I think 'John is through with me' now, what do you think? You know Hawthorne, your nickname ought to be 'butter,' 'cause you're all soft and yellow."

Luke realized suddenly that he was standing there without his pistols. Hawthorne's right hand started to twist around to draw his pistol from its butt forward position. In the act of turning his hand, Hawthorne heard, among the cheers, a double click followed closely by a third. He looked up into the double barrels of a Butler shotgun, held by Sing Loo, and a Winchester held by Henry.

"Don't do that," said Sing Loo.

"Yeah," said Henry. "We figured you'd be just enough of a snake in the grass to try something like this."

Hawthorne reined his horse around. In the process it went up on its hind legs and almost spilled him. He galloped out of the yard, followed by most of the rest of the Bar H men. A couple of them held back, arms out wide, indicating no hostile intent.

The fresh smell of new rain, as it fell on old dust, permeated the air. The rain was surprisingly cold for this time of year. There were tiny explosions of dust that erupted as the big drops hit the dry ground. The two Bar H men dismounted, and walked over to Fowler and brought him up to a sitting position. Luke walked over and squatted down. He looked Fowler in the eye.

Fowler looked at Luke and shook his head slowly, then he winced. "I've got to find a different line of work."

"Maybe just work for a different kind of man," said Luke.

Fowler looked around surprised. "Where'd they all go?"

Pete walked up, and handed Luke his pistols. "Hawthorne was going to shoot Luke while he was unarmed, but was talked out of it with a shotgun and a rifle. These two here are the only men who stayed behind to help you."

Fowler looked at them. "Yeah, they're friends of mine. Thanks for sticking around, boys."

Luke looked searchingly at the three men. "Let's all go into the barn and have a talk."

Fowler got up, very sore, and held his head very stiff as he walked. He buckled on his pistol that one of his companions had given him. He leaned against one of the stall posts. "I don't know why you two are being so decent to the likes of me."

"Maybe we weren't sure how deep you are in all of this, and wanted to give you the benefit of the doubt," said Pete.

"Probably a lot deeper than I ever wanted to be. I knew Dick had hired Sly, but I thought it was to scare you, not to murder anybody. I did a lot of bad things in my time, but murder ain't one of them."

"So what did you think when Sly and the boys came back the first day?" Pete asked.

"I wasn't happy about it, even though we were led to believe it was a fair fight, but I thought that what's done is done." Fowler looked at Luke. "No offense Luke, but we all thought the kid would sell the Circle D, since his dad was gone. Then the next day, when that torn up bunch came back carrying Sly, we figured that Pete here had gotten even. The bunch said that the boss of the Circle D had gunned down Sly, even when Sly tried to slicker him."

"Pete is the boss," Luke interjected.

"Yeah, well I can see how they might be confused," said Fowler, as he ruefully rubbed his head and jaw.

"Anyhow they couldn't draw their time, collect their gear, and light out fast enough. It didn't matter what Dick said, or how he cussed. They said Colorado seemed a lot healthier because if they stayed in Kansas, they were gonna be dead men. They said they'd seen rattlesnakes that struck slower than the boss of the Circle D. They were still just kind of babbling like that as they lit out. Zeb's face was swollen up, but he kept sayin' he'd stared death in the face, and didn't want no second chance."

The rain came down in a steady pour. There was an occasional flash of lightning, with an accompanying crack of thunder. Pete looked at Luke for a moment then back at Fowler. "What do you boys want to do now?"

Fowler said, "What do you mean?"

"Well, are you going back to the Bar H?"

"Only long enough to draw my time." John looked at his friends. The other two nodded in agreement. "I figure any boss who can't stick by one of his boys in a pinch, well, he ain't much of a boss, and not much of a man either."

"Why don't you boys stay here for tonight? We've got the best cook this side of the Mississippi," said Pete.

"Besides, it looks like this rain won't let up for a while," Luke added.

"Why, thanks, we'd appreciate it." Fowler shook hands with both men, and then they shook hands all around. "One thing I've been wondering." He looked at Pete.

"Yeah?"

He then looked back at Luke. "Luke, you shot George Sly." It was a statement not a question.

"That's right."

"Then did you beat the Bar H boys up too?"

Luke smiled. "No, that was Pete."

Fowler looked back at Pete. "Did you cut their clothes up, Pete?"

Pete smiled. "No, that was Rowdy."

"Well I swan, but the bunch of you sure put the fear in them boys somethin' fierce."

"We took all their blood money to give to Fury's next of kin. He was the hand that Sly murdered," Luke said.

"Oh, I see. That's why their clothes looked like they were cut up for doll rags. I didn't quite catch that when you mentioned it earlier. Things were a mite heated then." They all chuckled.

"Look, John, I'm sorry. I had no intention of fighting you, especially on your terms. I just got lucky."

"That wasn't luck. I've seen luck, and that ain't it. I hit at you where you weren't, and you hit me where I was. Several times. You're real quick too."

"Well thanks, but I was really trying to flush Hawthorne out, and make him stand or crawl."

"Oh, he showed yellow, I guess. Deep down, I always figured he might. I should have known it when you boys took a few long shots at us, and all Dick wanted to do was ride out fast. He talks real big, though."

Pete asked, "What do you think he'll do now?"

"He may try to find a few more gunmen. Sly was supposed to be the best around." No one commented. Fowler paused. "Do you really have his guns on the wall?" Luke gave a small smile and lowered his eyes, then he nodded his head. "Dang! That's something. When I realized it was you that beat Sly, I figured I was in for a tough time. I just didn't know how tough. Say, how many hands do you have?"

Pete looked at Luke then back at Fowler. "About twenty-four, why?"

"Aw, I don't know, I thought maybe you could use three more. You understand, it doesn't matter what your answer is. We ain't going back to the Bar H, except to draw our time." The other two again nodded their heads in agreement.

Luke said, "Sounds good to me. How many men does the Bar H have?"

"They had forty then they lost seven, one real permanent like, but then you know all about that. Now with the three of us gone it puts it down to thirty. He'll hire more though, he seems to have the money."

"Well," said Pete. "I don't know if we're doing you any favors, hiring you on. The odds may be long."

"Aw, heck, I don't care. For the first time in a long time, I like the side I'm on. I kind of like the odds."

Chapter Fourteen

Pete took John Fowler and the other two hands, Steve and Leroy, over to the bunkhouse to get them settled in. There was little grumbling among the Circle D hands. Mostly, they were curious. They found out that John had indeed been, among other things, a bare-knuckle fighter in various taverns, and elsewhere around the territory. He was tough, and his record had been a good one, even though prize fighting was supposedly illegal. However, it was not an occupation that he would relish going back to. His short run-in with Luke had convinced him of that. The Circle D hands had chuckled appreciatively, knowing that if it had been a straight bare-knuckle fight, the outcome might well have been different.

There was a lull for the next few days following the

Bar H visit to the Circle D. Fowler, and the two hands had ridden over to the Bar H to collect their gear and draw their time. Dick Hawthorne said, "Stick around, John, I've got some replacement hands coming. There's about five good gun hands in there too."

Fowler simply said, "No, thanks, it's time for us to be moving on."

He didn't say they were moving on to the Circle D. If he had said that, the discussion might have been longer and much more acrimonious.

Hawthorne thought, *I wonder why they've lost heart? Must be because of the beating that infernal kid gave him. Oh well, good riddance!*

Chapter Fifteen

The colonel was feeling better with each passing day. Sing Loo's awful smelling poultice and clear sleeping draught had done the trick. The colonel was up, and taking a step or two but Pete, Sing Loo, and Luke all wouldn't hear of him trying to ride just yet. In fact, they all threatened to slip him another of Sing Loo's special drinks if he did try to ride. Rowdy had taken seven other hands and ridden out to where the Bar H had tried to fence off Circle D and federal land. There were no new fence crews on the site. Rowdy and the boys tore down what little was left of the Bar H fencing efforts. Everyone knew this was only a lull in the conflict. If it was a truce, it was an uneasy one at best.

The days were lengthening, and the hands were working long hours in the saddle to round up the cattle for market. Circle D policy was that they ride only in a group of at least four men to avoid an ambush that might easily overwhelm one or two. Working in groups that large however, meant that they couldn't cover all the ground that they wanted. Some of the cattle were going missing, or maybe stolen. Luke had occasional glimpses of Dick Hawthorne's big white Stetson, but Hawthorne always seemed in a hurry to be somewhere else. "It's only a matter of time, Dick," Luke said to himself.

John Fowler fit in well with the Circle D. He had a self-deprecating type of humor, which everyone appreciated. In a talk with Rowdy he said, "I got my nose bent and these here eye scars for a real good reason. I was trying to block the punches to my stomach—with my face." Rowdy laughed appreciatively. Pete gave John the lead in a group of four and John had handled it well.

Some evenings, if they weren't too tired, Sing Loo, Henry, and Luke would work out in the barn. They might spar, with two men being the aggressor, or work out on the grain bags. Henry was learning a lot from Sing Loo and Luke. Luke taught him the stomach throw that he had used on Sloniker. "Be sure to put your foot crosswise, Henry," Luke said. "If you don't, your opponent could fall down on top of you. That's not where you want him."

Henry chuckled. When Henry used it to throw Luke into the hay, Sing Loo's response was, "Ah, good."

After being invited, John came over to watch. When he saw Luke do a familiar spin, hit, or kick he said, "Oh yeah, I remember that like it was yesterday. In fact, seeing that again makes me hurt all over."

As he said this he rubbed his jaw and head. He discovered after he had joined the workouts that Sing Loo could throw him as easily as he could anyone else. He soon learned the basic principles of Sing Loo's style of combat, and took to them like a duck to water.

Chapter Sixteen

Dick Hawthorne had not been idle. He sent word down to Dallas and over to Dodge City that he was looking for hands and paying fighting wages. He wasn't too particular how good a man might be with cattle; it was only his skill with guns that mattered. As might be expected, the quality of the new men was not the best. There were five genuine hardcases from Texas along with a couple of hangers-on. From Dodge, there were two drifters and one other. The third one smelled so bad even the seldom-washed cowhands wanted to stay up-wind of him. He was a taciturn man who kept to himself. With a nose smashed and a right ear cauliflowered, he was pretty easy to avoid. When asked how he should be addressed he growled, "Rube."

Since John Fowler had left, Dick Hawthorne didn't

118

have a lead hand. He didn't want to give the title of foreman to anyone, because that might usurp some of his own authority. He might also have to pay him more money and Hawthorne was cheap, among other things. From the new Texas hands, he selected Amos Albaugh to ramrod his takeover of the Circle D. Amos stood just under six feet. Everything about him spelled Texas, from his high Stetson hat, his red gambler shirt, his Levi pants, and custom boots, to his large rowel spurs. His black hair, brown eyes, dark swarthy skin, and flat nose indicated either some Mexican or Indian ancestry, maybe both. He had killed nine men in Texas and Mexico, four of them in fair fights, when there was no other way around it. He often bragged about the nine men he had killed, and was generally given a wide berth from the rest as a result. While the other men didn't particularly like him, he was generally accorded some respect because of his reputation. He and Rube Sloniker hated each other at first sight. Their relationship went downhill from there.

Amos and Dick sat down and planned their takeover of the Circle D. Dick promised a hefty bonus to all hands, especially Amos, when the job had been completed. There was no pretense that this dispute was about boundaries. Hawthorne was declaring out and out war. In the first two skirmishes, each side had had a man killed, but the head of the Circle D had also almost been killed. Hawthorne still cursed Sly's memory for not having completed the job. The last skirmish at the

Circle D had made Hawthorne look ridiculous. He was still smarting from Luke's taunts, and the fact that he had to turn tail and run. He would get even, if it was the last thing he would ever do.

In the previous week, Amos Albaugh had carefully scouted the land around the Circle D, looking for the best route and method of attack. The Circle D ranch house, and outlying buildings, were set on level ground with a wide view of the surrounding countryside. The barn and corrals were situated on the south and the bunkhouse and cook shacks were to the north. In between, and off to the side to form a large triangle, was the ranch house. He took note of the guards at night and laughed to himself. That would be the easy part.

Albaugh and Hawthorne agreed on a method of attack. Albaugh picked fifteen men to go with him on a raid of the Circle D. When he got to Rube Sloniker he ordered him along too. Rube demurred, saying, "I ain't going on a raid with the likes of you in charge. If Hawthorne wants to post me somewhere, that's okay, but I ain't goin' out on your sayso."

"You'll go if I say!" Amos hotly declared.

"Not on them big ol' spurs you're so all fired proud of, and if you don't like it you can just lump it. Besides, I like my Sharps, I ain't packin' a Winchester."

"You're supposed to be tough. From the looks of you it appears someone else is a whole lot tougher. Stay here if you're afraid."

Sloniker stood up, bigger than Amos Albaugh. His

filthy beard hung down stiff, his battered nose was purple, and his eyes were narrowed into slits. "I ain't afraid of nothin', I just don't like your plan, or you."

Finally Dick Hawthorne interrupted. "Rube, if you want to pack your Sharps, go ahead. You either go along on this raid, or light a shuck back to Dodge. I won't have any man who can't follow orders. I put Amos in charge, and that's the way it is."

"Fine, I'll go, and I'll take my Sharps."

"All right then, let's get to it," said Hawthorne. The "let's" was said with some license, since he had no intention of going on the raid himself.

Chapter Seventeen

Amos and Rube and fourteen others rode out well after dark toward the Circle D. When they got within a mile and a half of the ranch house, Amos signaled for a halt. Having asserted his authority, he really didn't care to have Rube in on the actual raid so he said, "Rube, you stay here and guard the horses. The rest of us will go in on foot. Okay?"

"That suits me just fine." Rube sneered as he stared at Amos.

The rest of the Bar H men had started advancing on foot. Amos took the lead and set a good pace. He allowed no talking. He signaled a halt about half a mile away from the ranch house. He advanced alone with a knife in his hand. He saw Steve, one of the former Bar H hands who was now with the Circle D. Steve, along with Leroy, was one of the two who had stayed with John Fowler after the fight with Luke. Steve was only 300 yards from the main house and yard. As Amos advanced through the tall stem grass, he inadvertently stepped on a piece of dry wood that made a snap.

Steve did not have to work the lever of his Winchester, he already had a cartridge in the chamber. Instead, he pulled the hammer from half-cock to full-cock with a small click in the night stillness. "Who's out there?" he called.

Amos couldn't get close enough to cut Steve's throat without being detected. Instead, he threw the knife from about eight yards. The Arkansas toothpick made a soft whispering sound as it did a complete turn in the air. The knife missed the intended target, the center of the chest, by three inches and, because of its shape, went deep into Steve's shoulder rather than his heart. Steve fell backward, and the butt of his rifle hit the ground, with his finger still on the trigger. The explosion of the rifle sounded like a stick of dynamite in the quiet of the night, but the bullet went harmlessly off in the air. Amos beckoned his men forward. Seven of them came with him. The other seven headed back for the horses, figuring to fight, maybe, another day.

As two of the Circle D guards crouched and started over, the other two held their ground, according to their emergency plan. Henry Bowen called out, "Steve, is everything okay?" There was no answer.

Henry heard, more than he saw, the group of eight

men running toward the barns, but he opened fire. Three of them turned around to answer with return fire, and Henry hit the ground trying to bury himself in the grass. Since it was night, the answering fire, though fierce, was high and wide. By now the Circle D hands had come boiling out of the bunkhouse. Most were only half dressed, some with only Stetsons, boots, and longjohns. All were armed with rifles however, and began pouring a running fusillade after the eight men. Two of the Bar H men managed to get close enough to the barns to throw torches into the hay. The hay was fresh cut, and therefore still damp, so only one of the fires caught and started burning the wood of one wall. A few of the Circle D hands split off, and got the fire out in short order. The rest of the hands took off after the Bar H hands who were now openly fleeing for their lives.

The first seven Bar H men had already mounted and left. Rube Sloniker kept the nine horses, counting his, ready for the remainder of them. As the second group mounted up, Rube took out his Sharps. He fired two shots at the Circle D pursuers. The second shot was unnecessary, because after the first big boom, everyone hit the ground including Luke and Pete.

"There's something about the sound of a Sharps that gives it some real authority," said Pete.

"Yeah," agreed Luke. "It usually means there's an ounce of lead flying by somewhere near. I've got a pretty good idea who might be on the other end of that Sharps."

They picked up Steve, who was still unconscious, and took him to the ranch house. Sing Loo took one look and stated the obvious, "The knife will have to come out." However, he didn't wait for any help. He took a firm grip and gently tugged the knife out. Steve came partially awake with a moan.

"Stop being a baby, or I will send you back to Bar H." With that, Steve mercifully sank back into unconsciousness, as Sing Loo cleaned and dressed his wound with a poultice.

Along with Leroy, John Fowler stood close by, feeling nothing but a cold anger. He turned to Luke. "When are we going to get some of ours back?"

"Tomorrow," said Luke. "They'll never guess what we're going to do."

When the Bar H hands rode back in that night, Dick Hawthorne was there to meet them, eager to hear the details of the raid. "What happened? How many buildings did you burn? How many of them did you kill? Did you get that infernal kid?" His blue eyes were dancing in anticipation, hoping for the quick demise of the Circle D.

Amos Albaugh swung out of the saddle. "It was a real mix-up. Things started off well enough, but then one of the guards heard us, and asked who was there. I got him with my knife, but he had his finger on the trigger of his rifle. When he fell back, the gun somehow went off. That roused up the Circle D men, but we kept going—leastwise, some of us did." He glared at the first group who had taken off. They stared back stubbornly.

Hawthorne ignored the tension. "Go on, go on, then what happened?"

"Well, we got in close enough to fire the barn, but it didn't look like it took. Leastwise, when we were leavin', I didn't see no flames."

Rube Sloniker interrupted. "You didn't see nothin,' 'cause you were too busy runnin' like a pack of dogs." Turning to Hawthorne he added, "If it hadn't been for me, and my big Sharps, they probably all would have been killed."

"Ah, what do you know? You were back by the horses, and didn't see nothin'," Amos jeered.

The rest of the hands had come out and were milling around, smoking and chewing, and talking in low tones. Clearly, this was not a good turn of events. To have been built up in strength to go on a punishing raid, and possibly only kill one man, and then hightail it back was a very bad sign. They remembered what had happened the last time that a Circle D hand had been killed. Anyone involved in the confrontation had been killed or humiliated, hurt, and run off.

"I saw enough to know that you don't know nothin'." Rube sneered. His stiff beard was wet with fresh tobacco juice, and his eyes glowed red. The cool night air did nothing to cover the stench of his unwashed body.

Hawthorne looked away in distaste. "All right. You

men take care of your horses. The rest of you get to bed, we've got work to do tomorrow. Amos come inside, I want to talk further with you." They talked long into the night.

Chapter Eighteen

The next day at the Circle D was a time of high tension and excitement. The hands were instructed to make a pretense of patrolling the area, but each group was told to stay in sight of another group. Every spare rifle and shotgun was gathered up on the ranch. It didn't matter what they were, wall-hanging flintlocks from long years past or muzzle loading shotguns, every one was taken to the ranch house. Then Luke collected every double-barreled shotgun he could find, seven in all, along with plenty of buckshot shells.

Pete and Tex took off early in the morning with a packhorse loaded with a curious cargo. They went south to the Arkansas River, then due west at a steady pace. If anyone had seen them, they would have called the look in their eyes purposeful, and their manner direct.

One of the Circle D hands nicknamed Arizona had taken a bad fall the previous day, and ended up with a bad limp. He was detailed to stay at the Circle D for the coming night. He was very unhappy, saying, "Aw shucks, I can still ride." All the rest of the Circle D hands were going on the raid. Thus only those unable to ride were at the Circle D ranch house.

They loaded every weapon on the Circle D, from the colonel's Spencer carbine, down to a Manton flintlock shotgun. There were also three extra Winchesters, compliments of the Bar H. All these weapons were strategically placed out of, or at, the windows in the ranch house and bunkhouse. They also made dummies out of old coats and hats which they placed sitting on chairs near the windows. Arizona moved a lamp with a low flame, limping at periodic intervals around the bunkhouse. In the main ranch house, the colonel, Maria, and Steve managed to keep up a good level of activity. Steve was still bedridden, but they gave him a string to pull a rocking chair with a dummy on it, a Winchester across its lap. The colonel still moved slowly, because of his wounds. There were only three guards posted on the perimeter but they were within 100 yards of the main compound. Everything was set for the coming evening.

Amos detailed three of his friends from Texas to scout the Circle D. They rode very carefully to within a mile of the perimeter and dismounted. It was getting dark and they crawled through the buffalo grass to within 300 yards of the compound. They saw constant movement inside the ranch house, and the bunkhouse. The windows were bristling with guns. The perimeter guards rotated at short intervals, keeping the Texas boys from any close up inspection. Every so often there was a big boom, from one of the guns in the windows. This was enough to put some realism into the whole made up scenario.

The three Bar H riders were led by Dusty, a Texan who was an unreconstructed rebel. He had killed a couple of carpetbaggers in Dallas. The fact that they were unarmed at the time hadn't mattered, it just seemed to Dusty that they needed killing. When the three rode in to the Bar H, Dusty was laughing.

Hawthorne and Albaugh met them on the front step. Dick looked up, his red face was shining. "Well, what happened? What does it look like over there?"

Dusty still had a smile. "It looks like they are ready for a long pitched battle, maybe even a siege. They got guards runnin' all over, and guns at every window. They even sent a shot whistling out our way. I don't think they really saw us though. They're acting real jumpy."

Dick and Amos both had smiles of satisfaction. "That's good they're scared, well, they got reason to be. Let's bed down tonight and think about what we're going to do to them tomorrow. Put out some guards, Amos."

Luke felt a little depressed. He knew that because of him some men were going to be dead tomorrow. He also knew that in a war of attrition, the Circle D was sure to lose. They had to make a bold stroke, not just a bold stroke but a smashing stroke. If it didn't go according to plan—his plan—then they would all be killed, or driven from the area.

Luke, and all the remaining Circle D riders, had taken a very wide route to the Bar H. The Bar H was well situated to withstand all the changes of weather, particularly the big winter blizzards with the resulting snowdrifts or the "blue norther" winds that would roar through with no warning. The main house was built up close to a bluff that was ninety feet high. The bluff extended for several hundred yards on either side. The bunkhouse was 100 yards to the north, also close to the bluff and adjacent to the cookhouse, and the barns and corrals were 200 yards east into the gently sloped valley. Led by Luke, twenty Circle D men rode to a small stand of cottonwood trees on the north side of the valley.

With them was their secret weapon, a little man all dressed in black named Sing Loo. Sing Loo had a small ten-inch tube of sewn leather filled with shot. In addition, he had two knives strapped to each leg, some thin rope, and a piece of wire. His job was to silently neutralize the sentries or, failing that, to kill them. Sing had insisted that he be allowed to come, and had suggested that he take out the Bar H men on watch. Luke knew that Sing Loo had the skill of stealth required for the job. What he wasn't sure was whether Sing Loo could kill in cold blood if necessary. Luke wasn't sure that he himself would be able to do that.

With that thought in mind, Luke put the question to him. "Sing, can you kill these men if you have to, without giving them a chance, without them even realizing that you are there?"

Sing Loo looked at Luke, brown eyes penetrating. He blinked once, as if to bring them in to sharper focus. He said nothing, only slowly nodded once, never breaking eye contact. Looking at Sing Loo, Luke shivered a little, even though it was before the cool of the evening.

The men waited under cover until dusk. Any talking that was necessary was done in whispers, and there was no smoking lest there be a telltale wisp spotted with a spyglass. As evening fell Sing Loo started into the grass. In his black outfit, he blended in with the countryside. Soon, he was invisible.

There were five Bar H hands on guard, two about 400 yards out and three 250 yards away from the main compound. The lateral distance between the guards was about 200 yards. The sun sank over the horizon, night fell quickly, and with it there was a sharp drop in temperature. While it was now spring, the Kansas winter was still not far behind. The Bar H guards were bundled up against the stiff breeze. They were facing outward, but hunkered down, Stetsons pulled low, and hugging their rifles like sweethearts at a barn dance on a Saturday night. The night was black, clouds swept across the face of the quarter moon, giving the landscape only brief glimpses of light.

Sing Loo crept well wide of the watching men, and came up behind the back of the far-flung group. Of the back line of three, he dispatched the first two with ease using his homemade cosh. The sound the cosh made as it hit their skulls was only slightly sharper than that of the wind whistling through the stem grass. Sing Loo hit them two, sometimes three times. If they didn't have concussions, it was only because of their extra thick heads. He made sure they would be unconscious for hours. He took the rifles off the men and put them up the back of their coats to keep them upright. Over the barrel ends he put their hats, so they were perched partially on their heads and the barrels.

The third man wasn't so lucky. He looked over at his chum to the right and something looked different to him. He just started to get up to walk over when Sing Loo took him silently from behind. As the man was rising, Sing Loo leaped on him the way he would leap on a horse just getting up out of the grass. He clamped his left hand over the man's mouth. With his right hand, the one with the knife in it, he slit the man's throat. The man fell forward, shuddered once, then lay still. He too was propped up, head forward, blood flowing down his front looking like a red bib. The last two were eliminated as easily as the first two had been. All four would have huge headaches, if they survived the night.

Sing Loo made it back to the stand of cottonwoods in short order, he didn't bother crawling. He looked at Luke. "It is done. No one is awake." His eyes stared directly at Luke, and if anything, they showed a pleasure at a job well done.

"Good, thanks Sing." Luke looked at everyone in his group. "Rowdy, Henry, you know what to do." They both nodded.

"The waiting is going to be the toughest part," whispered Rowdy.

"It's the most important part," said Luke. "There's going to be a lot of noise, but we have to do it right. There won't be a second chance. Each of you take three shotguns, we'll give Sing the last one, just in case. I know he can use it, he's killed enough game for the table." There was general agreement on that point. They all looked at one another and the silent thought hit home. This was a total Circle D effort. All the frustration and anxiety of the last few weeks were going to be resolved tonight, one way or the other.

Rowdy took a group of five men with him, and headed south. Henry did the same thing, only he went north. Both were heavy-laden groups since they were carrying extra longarms and ammunition. Sing Loo and two hands set up about 500 yards out from the main compound. They had three long paper cylinders with sticks on the back and fuses sticking out.

John Fowler walked over to Luke, the scars around his eyes showed vividly in the fleeting moonlight like small bright pieces of rope. Leroy was with him, and both men were carrying metal containers of coal oil, also known as kerosene, along with some rags and sticks for torches. "We appreciate your letting us come on the front of this raid, Luke." Leroy nodded in assent.

"Are you kidding, John? You two have the most dangerous part in the whole shebang. Frankly, if we get out of this thing whole, I'll be more than happy."

Leroy smiled and John chuckled. "Well now I ain't one to point fingers but it is your plan and, if I say so myself, a darn good one."

"Let's hope so," Luke said a little nervously, yet feeling somewhat relieved at John's confidence in him. "As near as I can tell, it looks like the others are in place, shall we get to it?"

"Yep, let's open the ball."

Luke felt a little madness at the idea of impending combat. His blood was starting to sing. This was their battle; they were righting a wrong. John, Leroy, Luke, and two others were in the group heading in toward the compound. Sing Loo impassively watched them file by, and then spread out. They walked unhurriedly, but crouched down. The poleaxed guards of the Bar H made no movement whatsoever as the group walked by them. Luke noticed the guard on the far right at the back of the Bar H guard contingent. It looked like he had a big smile, but it was too far down to show any humor. Then they saw the blood. Luke looked at John who was also transfixed by the ghoulish exhibit and both of them showed sickly smiles of their own. The grass made a soft whooshing sound as they walked through it. The breeze was turning into a wind, as the night grew colder. They all shivered, but not just from the cold.

Luke's group approached on a direct line with the barn. There was little chance they would be spotted from the ranch house. John and Leroy got busy dousing the far outside wall of the barn with coal oil. They also made four torches. Luke, and one other hand, went into the barn and opened up all the horse stalls. Then they propped both ends of the barn open, as John and Leroy ignited the barn wall. Torches were thrown in through the upper opening, only one doing damage, as it found a pile of dry hay.

The first thing any of the Bar H hands heard was the sound of the horses milling around out by the corral. Dusty looked out and saw his favorite horse, a big black stallion from Tennessee, galloping out into the valley. He swore, and woke the others up with a holler. "Hey, the horses are out!"

The hands raced out of the bunkhouse, only to be met by rifle fire from Luke and his group. One hand was killed outright, one was severely wounded and a third suffered a broken leg after he tripped and was run over by the stampeding Bar H hands running back into the bunkhouse.

Outside, all was pandemonium. The fire had now reached the roof of the barn. It would soon be a total loss. Luke, John, and the others were still firing rapidly at the bunkhouse and the ranch house. As they fired, they worked the levers of their rifles with machine-like efficiency. While firing, they moved, from side to side and ducked, to avoid becoming stationary targets. The impact of the rifle fire sounded like a hammer rapidly being beaten against the bunkhouse wall. More often than not, the bullets would penetrate one wall, sometimes two. The splinters from the dry bunkhouse wall whirled around like small tornadoes, embedding in some of the Bar H men's exposed flesh, and hampering their aim. In this exchange, two more Bar H men were killed. In spite of all this, the Bar H was starting to organize. Led by Amos and Dusty, they put up a convincing wall of gunfire.

Amos yelled above the din of explosions and ricochets, "Everybody, grab a gun, we're going out after them. They'll cut us to pieces if we stay in here." In varying stages of dress, they began to run out in groups of two, alternating left and right once outside the door.

Luke saw the Bar H come out, and waved his group back. The Circle D ran out by the burning barn. As they went past the barn, a crescendo of crackling flames and searing heat combined in an explosion to bring the roof down as it collapsed into the inferno. The sparks shot 100 feet into the air, and whirled in the wind, creating a gigantic pyrotechnic display. After running another fifty yards, they were by the first line of Bar H guards. They stopped by the two still unconscious men, and turned around. Luke and John had the same idea, as they tugged the rifles out of the backs of the guard's coats. Luke looked across the expanse of grass at John, then they both looked at the advancing Bar H led by Dusty. They leveled their rifles and all five men fired. Dusty came to an abrupt halt, it looked as if he had run into a stone wall. One second he was running full speed, the next he was flat on his back dead.

Bullets were singing by Luke and John, and their little group. Through the air the bullets made a whine, in the grass, they were more of a whir, like an insect that has lost its way. Unfortunately for the sleeping Bar H guards, crouching and firing near them provoked a different sound. Luke heard two thuds, as Bar H bullets hit the back of one trussed-up guard. The guard literally never knew what hit him.

Chapter Nineteen

At the sound of the first gunshot, Dick Hawthorne rolled out of bed and lay on the floor. He got up, and peered out of the bedroom window, but ducked down again, as a bullet came crashing through the window and out the other wall. His breathing was fast, and his heart was going like a steam locomotive on a downhill run. He saw his barn going up in flames, and while he was enraged, he felt a grudging admiration. "Now that's how a barn ought to be burnt." He grabbed his Winchester rifle and fired a few times at the fleeing shadows. Dusty and Amos were leading the rest of the hands on the chase, Hawthorne was slow to join them.

"My guards, where are my guards?" Hawthorne cried.

As the Bar H hands spread out and moved forward, Hawthorne emerged from the ranch house at a slow trot. Without thinking, he put on his big white Stetson. He led bravely from the rear, exhorting his hands, "Go get 'em boys, don't let 'em get away."

Behind the Bar H, ninety feet above on the bluff, crouched in buffalo grass, Pete and Tex surveyed the battle scene with extreme satisfaction. While it was very tempting to potshot Dick Hawthorne as he straggled at the rear of his men, that might give away their position, and consequently, their mission. They had traveled most of the day, taking a big circle route down by the Arkansas River then north to the west of the Bar H. They had hidden in the late afternoon in a stand of trees five miles to the west of the Bar H. Between Pete and Tex there was complete understanding but due to Tex's reticence, almost no conversation. With the arrival of evening, they had completed their journey to the top of the bluff overlooking the Bar H. They crawled up to the edge of the bluff, and awaited further events. It was difficult to see in the night. It appeared there was a slight movement by one of the back Bar H guards, but that's all they could tell.

"Well, let's get to it," Pete softly said.

"Yup," Tex replied.

They brought the packhorse up, and unloaded part of its cargo. This portion of the load consisted of five bladders, filled with coal oil sealed with wax, and ten sticks of dynamite. In addition, they brought a bow and arrows, and some rags. The dynamite sticks were attached to some of the arrows. Pete rode his horse, and led the packhorse 100 yards north to the area above the bunkhouse. He kept well away from the rim, lest he be spotted from down below. Once there, over the bunkhouse, with the cookhouse next to it, he unloaded the rest of his cargo, which was similar to the first load. Pete proceeded to lay out his material as Tex was doing, except that he had nine bladders and fifteen sticks of dynamite plus a bow and arrows. Many of the dynamite sticks were attached to the bottom of an arrow, with the fuses pointing backward.

Pete looked down at Tex, and held his hand up high in the air. Tex returned the signal. Both men proceeded to drop the first of their bladders ninety feet down onto the roofs. The fifteen-pound bladders hit with a loud splat, and disgorged their contents all over the roofs. They thought initially that two bladders per roof would suffice. After throwing the bladders, Pete and Tex wrapped the end of some arrows with rags soaked in coal oil. The coal oil odor was pervasive and blotted out all other smells. They lit the rags, then shot them into the roofs, which began to blaze up immediately. After allowing the roofs to burn for about three minutes, they threw another bladder onto each roof. These had the effect of cutting off the fires from oxygen and making them subside, but only for a moment, then the fires flared up again, this time twice as intensely as before.

A few minutes later, Tex shot an arrow with a stick of dynamite into the roof of the ranch house. Pete did the same thing to the bunkhouse and cookhouse. Both of the men had to retreat from the edge of the bluff, about twenty yards back, after gathering up the remaining dynamite. In fact, they ran. The ensuing explosions blew part of the roofs down inside the buildings. The other parts were blown up and out over the surrounding area. Some of the burning debris flew up as high as the bluff top, but didn't do any damage there. Pete and Tex ran back to their respective stations. They threw the remaining bladders into the now open jaws of the buildings, where the roofs used to be. The coal oil created a fiery inferno which before had been confined to the roofs. The stored ammunition in the ranch house was burning, and crackled like someone crumpling up a gigantic piece of paper.

Luke, John, and Leroy and the other two hands ran another 150 yards back to the other two unconscious Bar H guards. All of them turned around, and loosed another fusillade at the pursuing Bar H men. Luke looked back toward Sing Loo, he hoped that Sing could see him in the night gloom. At that instant, and only for an instant, a sliver of light shone from the quarter moon through the swift moving clouds. Luke took off his hat and waved it high in the air in big circles.

"Ah, good," Sing Loo said.

Sing Loo lit the three skyrockets in rapid succession. The thick red trails arched high in the air. At that point, the Bar H hunters became the hunted. Luke and John and the rest ran the remaining 100 yards back to Sing

Loo and the other two Circle D hands, then turned around and waited.

Along with their own rifles, Luke and John had brought four extra Bar H rifles back with them. Luke gave one to John, and one to Leroy, the other he gave to Sing Loo to go along with his shotgun. The last one, he kept.

"Quickly, I want everyone at ten-yard intervals. Wait until you hear the shotgun go off, then open up with everything you've got. John, you take the north end. Leroy, you take the south end. Okay?" They both nodded.

"All right, everybody load up and wait for the shotgun."

They spread out, all eight of them, crouched down in the high buffalo grass, then they rapidly reloaded their weapons and waited. Luke, John, and Leroy and the other two hands were all sweating and excited from their recent exertions. Sing Loo and the remaining two Circle D hands were rested, but still excited.

Amos was leading the rest of the Bar H hands, still over thirty in number. He stopped momentarily to look at Dusty, who was sprawled out in death. Rather than any particular sympathy, he felt a momentary apprehension. "Why hasn't the Circle D ridden out by now? They've burned our barn, and turned the horses loose. There's no way we could catch them." More rifle fire erupted from the Circle D group, the bullets went singing by Amos. "Let's go boys, get 'em," Amos yelled. About that time, the rockets went off.

After seeing the signal rockets, Henry led his five men straight in from the north in a ninety-degree flanking movement. He spread the men out only three yards apart. He carried one of their three allotted shotguns, along with his Winchester. "Don't anybody shoot until I do, or unless one of them spots us."

A few hundred yards away, Rowdy led his men down the south side of the valley. They had hidden in the grass until the Bar H men had gone by. His men were set up to block the Bar H men when they started to retreat, but Rowdy was given the most latitude in his instructions. "Whatever you think best to do the most damage, do it," Luke said.

Rowdy and his five men moved in, still staying low. They didn't want to get shot by their own men. Seeing the rockets, he said in a low growl, "All right boys, we get 'em when they turn back or when I fire."

He too had appropriated one of the shotguns, dispensing the other two to his men. Placing his men at five-yard intervals, Rowdy took the last spot, the one closest to the action, for himself. They started to close in, like the far end of the pincer of a crab, still holding their fire.

Amos and the Bar H hands paused by the first row of guards. They realized that they had probably killed their own man, with two bullets in the back, but they looked at it as the luck of the draw. The group that saw the guard farthest north had a different view. When they saw the big cut across his throat and his macabre smile, they shuddered. A few wanted to turn back. It took Amos sprinting up to them and exhorting them, to keep them going.

"C'mon you men, we got 'em, we got 'em on the run. Let's go kill 'em."

"Yeah?" one of them exclaimed doubtfully, gesturing at the rockets. "Then why does it look like they're celebrating the Fourth of July?"

The Bar H men got to within seventy yards of Luke and the other seven men of the Circle D. "Now, Sing," Luke yelled.

Sing Loo let loose with a blast from his American Arms shotgun. Although they were seventy yards away, the buckshot cut down two of the Bar H men. Luke and the rest poured in rifle fire at a fast rate, and accounted for another three. The return fire killed the Circle D hand next to Sing Loo and Leroy took a slug in the side, doing a pirouette as he went down.

Only a couple of Bar H men had had the presence of mind to grab a box of shells when they went chasing after the Circle D hands. Amos wasn't one of them. Many of the Bar H rifle hammers were now falling on empty chambers.

"Grab the guns of the ones who're down. Get some more shells from these two men," Amos yelled.

Henry led his men in a right flanking movement to within thirty yards of the Bar H men. The whole attention of the Bar H hands was taken with trying to kill Luke and his small group. They were milling around, trying to re-arm, reload and regroup.

One of the Bar H men glanced over to his left, saw Henry's group, and let out a strangled cry, "Look out, over there!"

Henry fired his double-barreled shotgun, closely followed by the rest of his group. Two more shotguns and two Winchesters erupted in a concentrated fire into the condensed left flank of the Bar H men, the results predictable yet terrible. The six barrels of buckshot cut a bloody swath through the Bar H, killing eight men outright and wounding six more, two of them fatally. Rifle fire, from this quarter, accounted for two more dead of the Bar H. Seeing the shocking effect of the shotgun fire, Henry reloaded and fired again and again. The blasts didn't have the same telling effect this time, but they still killed two more of the Bar H hands.

Amos took two buckshot balls in the right arm which rendered it useless. A third ball lodged in his neck. He dropped his rifle, all thoughts of continuing the battle gone. Cradling his wounded arm, and half blinded with pain, he lurched as he turned around to get away.

Having left one man, Sing Loo, to tend to Leroy, Luke and the rest of his men got up and started forward, with fully loaded Winchesters. They poured a concentrated fire into the Bar H hands, who were still standing, many with empty weapons. Between Luke's and Henry's groups, they killed four more. At that point they heard the dynamite explosions.

"C'mon," Luke yelled. Then, blood maddened, he let out a high pitched keening yell, like a cougar that had just killed its dinner. In the telling of the story, in later years by people who were there or who only wished they were, this was the defining point of the battle, Luke's vision was blurred, and he was in a fury as he charged. The remaining ten men of the Bar H turned and fled for their lives, their only thought being speed, with Amos bringing up the rear. He was still holding his arm, tilting his head at an odd angle, and bleeding.

Chapter Twenty

From 150 yards back, Dick Hawthorne turned around in total stupefaction at the sound of the dynamite. He hadn't noticed the other burning buildings because of the blazing inferno of the barn. The ten fleeing men from the Bar H came up behind him, and stared at the devastation, two of them holding Amos up. Now, there was nowhere they could go, and nothing that they could retreat to, and be safe. This round of fighting was over; they'd been knocked flat. Hawthorne was going to have to hire some more men, and figure a different way of attacking the Circle D. It would take some doing, but Hawthorne figured he could be back within two or three months. He knew of some gunmen in Wichita and Abilene. His men looked back, and wondered why the Circle D men were advancing on the south side of the valley only. Then they looked the other way, and knew why. Rowdy and his group were advancing only fifty yards away from the west, the rest of the Circle D didn't want to get caught in the crossfire. Rowdy stopped, only ten yards away.

Dick Hawthorne, having intentionally stayed in the rear, suddenly was exactly where he didn't want to be in the fight, out in front. He had his rifle in his left hand. Imperiously, he held his right hand, palm out, toward Rowdy, "Now you just hold on there, you just hold on."

Rowdy was enjoying himself, he wasn't going to miss out after all. His lively blue eyes were dancing. "What should I hold on for, Hawthorne?"

Still thinking only of himself, Hawthorne replied, "You just let me surrender, I'll talk to that Dawson kid, we'll work all this out." He dropped his rifle and held out his left hand but he dropped his right hand to his pistol. Still looking for an opening he started to back up, hopeful of getting behind his remaining men.

Drawing a bead on Hawthorne with his shotgun, Rowdy offered, "Why sure Hawthorne, anybody still standing, we might let 'em surrender."

"No, please. I'll pay you, I'll do anything."

"Hawthorne, you have done enough. You sowed the wind, and now you're gonna reap the whirlwind."

All Rowdy's men's weapons were aimed at Hawthorne, and while Rowdy pulled his triggers first, the others weren't a half second behind. At that short range the explosions were deafening. The buckshot killed Hawthorne. His white Stetson flew up in the air, full of holes, and with a large piece missing. Hawthorne was blown back eight feet. The two Bar H hands having the bad luck to stand directly behind Hawthorne were also killed in the gunfire. The rest, including Amos Albaugh, had the good sense to throw themselves painfully to the ground, while Hawthorne was begging for his life.

As luck would have it, Rube Sloniker was not in the bunkhouse when the shooting started. His anti-social behavior, along with his foul, rancid smell, convinced Hawthorne to order Rube to sleep outside. This was no particular hardship, since Rube had slept outdoors most of his life. He didn't like the way he was being treated, though. As far as he was concerned, he'd been the hero of the raid on the Circle D. Not only did he get no credit for saving the rest of the hands on the raid, he still hadn't been paid. He took all of his gear, and rolled into his buffalo robes, finding cover in a stand of trees about fifty yards north of the bunkhouse. The night was cool verging on cold, but Rube would have been comfortable even if it were fifty degrees colder. He put his horse on a long rope, allowing it to graze. The first sign he had that anything was wrong was when he heard the shots being fired at the bunkhouse. Rube rolled out of his robes, and grabbed his Sharps rifle. He could see the Circle D men in the light of the barn fire. Rube drew a bead on one, and then he hesitated. He didn't see why he should shoot. After all, what did it get him the last time? This time it might get him shot, so he awaited further developments.

Rube watched as the battle unfolded. It looked like the Bar H was going to drive the Circle D back. Then he heard the loud splats on the roofs of the bunkhouse and cookhouse. He observed the fire arrows with utter disbelief. He made his decision long before the dynamite went off. Later, when it did, he swore long and fluently. He knew he was leaving as broke as he was when he came.

"Well, looks like I ain't gonna get paid anyhow. There ain't gonna be any big bonus, either," Rube said to himself.

Rube saddled up his horse and stowed his gear. However, he had a great idea on how to overcome his poverty. He managed to drive four of the released Bar H horses in front of him, as he headed up north, away from the area of combat. He might have been able to get more horses, but he was anxious not to be seen by anyone from the Circle D.

"After all that, I may be the only one who comes out ahead. These here horses ought to cover my pay, and then maybe some of that bonus." Rube laughed. He headed the horses farther northward into the night and away from the fight.

Chapter Twenty-one

Rowdy got the surviving Bar H hands on their feet. They were shaken at the suddenness of the encounter and at Hawthorne's death, and were queasily trying to clean themselves. Amos, and now two others, were in so much pain that they didn't care, they just wanted to lie down. Joe Lowe was the only Texas hardcase still standing, all the other Texans had been either killed or badly wounded. He walked over to Amos and squatted down. "Well, Texas is sure lookin' good."

Amos grimaced. "That's the next stop I want to make, if they ever let us out of this."

Luke, Henry, John, and Sing Loo came walking up, along with some of the Circle D hands. Luke had sent the others back to retrieve their horses. "Good job, Rowdy, anybody hurt?"

152

"Nobody on our side."

"Is that Hawthorne?"

"Yeah, what's left of him," Rowdy said.

"He's looked better," John wryly observed. "Bet he won't be tryin' to backshoot nobody no more."

Out of forty Bar H men there were seven left standing. The rest were wounded, dead, or, like in Rube Sloniker's case, deserted. Luke looked at Joe Lowe. "You the ranking one left now?"

"Yeah, since Amos there is hurt, I reckon."

Luke indicated a flat spot in the grass. "Gather all the weapons around here, and put them there, including yours."

"Well now—" Joe started to protest.

"Joe," Amos rasped. Joe walked back over and knelt down. "Do what he says. He's the one that got Sly."

With no further comment, Joe stood up, unbuckled his gunbelt, and threw it in the spot indicated by Luke. "Let's go everybody, you heard the man."

There was a general clinking and clanking as the few remaining Bar H hands complied. They were instructed to get their wounded together, and to help them as much as possible. The three "sleeping" guards finally came awake, which made ten Bar H hands who could walk, maybe not steadily, but they could walk.

The wounded were brought over fairly near the barn, so they could be seen and aided in the glow of its fire. Three shovels and a pick were salvaged from an adjacent shed, and the Bar H hands were put to work digging graves. They dug near the copse of trees where Rube had spent some of the night. During the night, five of the remaining nine Bar H wounded died.

Amos managed to hold on until Sing Loo got to him. At first, he was frightened of the little man in black, with the knives in his hand. However, Sing Loo very gently probed, and removed all the buckshot, including the one in his neck. The only antiseptic available was some whisky. Sing Loo gave it to Amos saying, "Here, drink." After that, it didn't hurt quite as much when Sing Loo poured the rest of the whisky in the wounds. Sing Loo had first taken care of Leroy, and sent him back to the Circle D. The other hand, Will Morgan, was sent back over his saddle to be buried on Circle D land alongside Fury.

An hour after the shooting stopped, Pete and Tex rode in, still smelling of coal oil. Their packhorse had a much smaller load than when they had started out. "If this doesn't look like Atlanta after the march, I'll buy the sasparilla," exclaimed Pete.

"Yup," Tex added.

Luke and John rode up. Henry came in from a different direction. All of them had extra weapons cradled in their arms, which they dumped unceremoniously onto the ground with the others already there.

"We could always open a Circle D gunshop. There's enough stock here to give it a good start," laughed Pete.

"You sure did a great job up there, Pete and Tex,"

said Luke. "Showing 'em they had nothing to retreat to sure took the starch out of 'em."

"It was your plan, Luke. Where'd you get it? The Book of Joshua, you said?"

"Yep, the eighth chapter."

"Well, it worked to perfection," said Pete.

"Almost," Luke added somberly. "We lost Will Morgan and Leroy took one in the side. Sing thinks he's going to be okay though."

"It's too bad about Will. We'll get some money to his next of kin. I'm glad to hear Leroy is going to be all right," said Pete.

"Me too. Him and Steve were the only ones that stuck by me, when everyone else from the Bar H hightailed it," added John Fowler.

"I'd say the Bar H is through," Pete said. "They got a lot more dead than alive, and the ones that are alive ain't moving all very well."

The fighting madness had left Luke. Now he felt only a melancholy sadness as he surveyed the unnecessary waste that had been the Bar H. The biggest legacy of the Bar H wouldn't be crossbred cattle, or thoroughbred horses, unfortunately, it would be the graveyard with many of the occupants unnamed. The Circle D hands who weren't guarding the Bar H men had ridden back home, having worked through most of the night. Luke rode over to the still smoldering ranch house, and dismounted. One corner was still standing though the rest was level. The far end of the house was blown out where the ammunition had been stored.

John Fowler rode up and dismounted by Luke. "You know I heard rumors about what might have been in that corner, but I never saw anythin'."

"Like what?" Luke asked.

"We heard Dick had him a big old safe that was built into the house, and that nobody could figure how to get in it."

Now Luke was curious. "Why don't we just have us a look see?"

"Let's move all the Bar H hands up north of the graveyard. No need for them to see what's going on," Pete offered.

"Good idea, Pete," Luke agreed.

After they had moved the Bar H men with the accompanying groans of the wounded, Pete, Luke, and John went to work. Rowdy, Tex, Henry, and Sing Loo kept a watch out for anyone who might get curious. The ranch house was still smoldering in places, but the fire had burned itself out for the most part, while up north, the cookhouse was still burning. Pete threw a wide loop over the corner area of the ranch house, catching it on the jagged pieces of burnt wood. He wrapped the rope around his saddle horn and backed his horse up, like he had a straining bull on the end of it. The whole outer wall came down with a crash, exposing an inner wall of metal that completely surrounded whatever was inside of it.

"That looks like the outside to some kind of vault," Luke said. "How do we get inside that?"

"We can open this up like a can of peaches, same way we did the roof." Pete laughed.

With that, he walked over to the packhorse and retrieved a stick of dynamite. Using his Bowie knife, Pete cut the stick in half then inserted the cap and fuse. He cleared away some of the debris at the bottom of the metal wall, then dug out a space with his knife, and put the half stick in. He timed the fuse for about a minute. Pete lit the fuse, then retreated about thirty yards, to join Luke and John. The explosion was a low boom, somewhat muffled by the surrounding debris. After a moment's hesitation, the front and side walls collapsed with a crash. The top and back walls of the structure were resting on the now exposed fireproof safe.

"Well, well, well, just look at what we've got here," exclaimed Luke.

"I heard rumors about this," John said. "I didn't know until right now that they were true."

Sing Loo, Rowdy, Henry, and Tex had all come closer to gaze at the safe, not worrying about the Bar H men, or what was left of them, being curious. They no longer posed a threat.

Pete brought out another stick of dynamite, and cut it in half. He prepared each half to explode, then attached them to the upper and lower hinges of the door to the safe. The fuse he cut into as exact two lengths as he could, then he lit them, and everybody scattered. The explosions were almost, but not quite, simultaneous. They did have the salutary effect of blowing the door off its hinges, and consequently off the safe.

Inside the safe, the dust was still settling, but there were no loose items to be lost. Packed securely were many heavy canvas bags in a large pile, most were plain, but three were marked Wells Fargo and Company.

"Well," said Pete, "it looks like old Dick didn't depend on the ranch business for his living."

Luke grabbed the Wells Fargo bags and opened them. Inside were a few letters and bunches of new bank notes with the Wells Fargo name on the bands. Some of the new note bundles were dated back to 1869. The other bags held loose gold and silver coins and two bags were filled with smaller leather sacks containing five pounds each of raw gold dust.

"It's no wonder that he had all the money he needed to fight us," said Luke. "What I don't understand is why he felt like he had to take us on."

"Human nature, Luke," Pete explained. "Dick had to be the big dog in the meathouse. It didn't matter none that he had a lot of money, regardless where he got it. He wanted to control the whole shebang, and the Circle D was in his way. What he didn't count on was that the Circle D wouldn't get out of his way."

"I guess what Rowdy said to him out of the Book of Hosea was dead spot on," Luke said.

"You mean about the wind and whirlwind?"

"Yes."

"Rowdy was right," Pete added. "If he hadn't shot him, we'd have had to hang him, sooner or later. There wasn't any way that Hawthorne wasn't going to try to take over the Circle D again. The next time might have had a different result, or at least a lot bloodier one."

"Hey John," Luke asked, "did you know anything about any of this? You were with Hawthorne almost a year."

John looked at the canvas sacks, and shook his head. "I saw different strangers riding in and out, mostly at night. Dick was gone a few days at a time, but I never knew anything about this. There was that rumor about this safe, though."

"Let's get all this material packed up on a couple of horses," Luke said. "If you can find any other items that might be of importance, get them too."

Henry kicked through some of the smoldering debris. "Anything outside the safe is ashes."

"You're probably right, Henry," Luke said, "Keep looking for a bit though, and see if anything turns up. Pete, John would you ride up to the trees with me, I want to give the rest of the Bar H a farewell."

Pete and John chuckled as they mounted up, wanting to see what Luke had next in mind. Luke stopped over at the pile of Bar H weapons, and picked out three of the most worn pistols, all conversions to cartridge from percussion. He also picked out some belts, and eighteen rounds of ammunition, for each pistol. The three then rode slowly up to the Bar H hands. A cold dawn was now upon them, replacing the colder night.

Joe Lowe was supervising the last internment of the Bar H hands. He looked up as the three rode up. Luke, Pete, and John all ignored him. There were four Circle D hands, all armed with shotguns, guarding the Bar H as they went about their tasks. Two more wounded had died in the night, and they too had joined their companions in the ground. Now there was only one hand with a broken leg, Amos Albaugh with an arm and neck wound, and ten other hands.

Luke addressed himself to the leader of the four guards, a big redheaded kid from Iowa named Carl Thorpe, "How'd it go?"

"Fine Luke, the one fellow over there was making noises like he thinks he's tough," Carl said, indicating Joe Lowe.

"Carl, take Dwight with you and round up twelve of the sorriest nags you can find of Bar H stock. See if you can find any tack in what's left of the shed. Otherwise, bring some rope. They can make some bridles with that."

"What about saddles?" Carl asked.

"They're lucky to be alive," Luke replied. "If there are any blankets they can use them for saddles, but if you find any saddles, keep 'em."

Joe Lowe just had to show how salty he was. Hearing

the previous conversation between Luke and Carl had made him decidedly more unhappy. He'd been digging all night, mad and frustrated at his circumstances, so he threw caution to the wind and spat out, "You all are real tough with guns on. I'd like to see how any one of you would do with me, man to man."

Pete started to take his guns off and dismount, but John interjected. "Now hold on there, Pete. As you may recall I ain't won too many lately. In fact, the last time I commenced to do just what you're doing, the only luck I had at all was bad. I just naturally got to try and change it."

Pete chuckled, settled back on his horse, and Luke laughed out loud. Carl and the other Circle D hands chortled. Of the Bar H hands still living, few had heard of John Fowler. None of them knew until now that he was working for the Circle D. Joe Lowe was about the same size as John. Joe was rangy, and had had several fisted encounters, in which he had been successful. He showed no fear of John Fowler. John himself felt no fear, only curiosity, thinking, *I wonder if I can make this stuff of Sing Loo's really work for me.*

John unbuckled his gunbelt, wrapped it around his saddlehorn, and turned around. As John advanced, Joe wondered about the scars about John's eyes, even so, he set himself, and threw a looping right hand. John grabbed his arm with his left hand and quickly pivoting, ran his right arm around Joe's waist. John then lifted Joe up in a hip toss and slammed Joe to the ground.

"Aw heck," John said, "that's too easy, c'mon and get up."

Joe scrambled to his feet, and warily advanced. This time he threw a couple of rapid lefts, which John easily parried. He threw another left, and caught John high on the head. John winced.

"C'mon John, quit playin' around," Luke catcalled.

John gave Luke a wry grin, then advanced. Joe fired a hard left, but it stayed out a fraction of a second too long. John ducked then came up and over the left with a tremendous looping right cross to Joe's left temple. Joe staggered back, John followed in with a double left hook to the jaw. John threw another right which caught Joe on the cheek and eye. Joe raised his hands to protect his head, and John followed up with three piston-like strikes to the belly. Joe bent over, and John felled him with another straight right to the jaw. Joe collapsed into unconsciousness.

"Dang, that felt good," exclaimed John while flexing his arms and shoulders.

Led by Luke, the Circle D cheered. Not for the first time did Luke realize just how lucky he had been in his own encounter with John Fowler.

Amos Albaugh leaned back, groaned, and closed his eyes in pain muttering, "That boy just doesn't learn."

A few bridles were salvaged from the shed. The saddles were put in a different area. Per Luke's instructions, rope was provided to make the remaining bridles. Luke relented about the saddles, however, allowing the badly wounded Amos Albaugh to have one and the man with the broken leg, another. As for the rest, he said, "You all can just ride bareback. That's where you do most of your thinking anyway, on your backsides. Remember the ending to this fight, next time you want to hire your guns out."

"When do we get our guns back?" one of the former Bar H hands hopefully asked.

"You don't," said Luke confirming their worst fears. "You have three pistols with eighteen rounds of ammunition each for the twelve of you. If anyone wants to continue the war with those, well, have at it."

"There ain't enough ammunition there to go huntin' prairie dogs," the Bar H hand complained.

"That's about right," Luke agreed. "Now, get your unconscious friend here up, and ride out all of you. Consider yourselves lucky we don't hang the lot of you which, if we had the inclination, we have every right to do."

With nothing left to say, the twelve former Bar H men mounted up, slowly and painfully, in some cases. They headed out in a group, plodding toward Dodge City, which was the closest place they could go, to find some support for any further journey. Having seen the total destruction of the Bar H, and the violent death of

Dick Hawthorne, even the dullest of them realized that there was no reason to return. They also realized that with the little armament available to them that they had better stick together.

Chapter Twenty-two

Luke, Pete, and the rest headed back to the Circle D. The only things left of the Bar H were some burnt-out buildings and a graveyard. In the coming days, Luke would send out men to round up all the Bar H stock and drive it over to the Circle D. There was no sense letting the stock fend for themselves, starve, or be taken by marauders who might pass by.

Luke would keep the patrolling groups of no less than four men each for the time being. He wanted to be ready for possible retaliation, from any unexpected area.

Pete put a couple of hands to work cleaning and oiling all the captured weapons, of which there was quite an array. The Circle D hands were allowed to upgrade their weapons in any way they saw fit, or to take as many as they wanted to pack. Many pistols disappeared in this way, as an extra carry weapon or hide out gun.

The canvas sacks presented a different kind of dilemma. Luke had all of the sacks delivered to the front room of the Circle D ranch house. The colonel had been thoroughly briefed on the details of the battle and he congratulated the men on a well-executed plan. He sat down on the couch, carefully, as he was still tender from his wounds, and surveyed the pile of sacks.

"The plan was all Luke's," said Pete. Everyone else nodded in assent.

"Without everyone having the nerve to carry it out, it would have just been so much paper," Luke modestly proclaimed. "And Sing? Well, Sing's got more guts than any three normal men. Dad, the way he took out those guards, so quick and silent."

Everyone started talking at once—Pete, John, Henry, and Rowdy. Tex chimed in with an occasional "yep" and Sing Loo smiled, with an added "heh, heh" or "ah, good." While not as formal as an after action report, the conversations were very enlightening, and the colonel again let everyone know how proud he was of them, and how he regretted not being in on the action himself. Luke and Sing Loo looked at each other. The colonel, along with recovering from his wounds, was also starting to regain his energy.

"Let's take a look at these sacks," the colonel said.

Luke pulled out the three Wells Fargo sacks, and opened them. The letters were of internal Wells Fargo correspondence, one sack dating back to 1869, another, 1872, and a third, 1875, the current year. The new bills dated the same years totaled $48,000. The rest of the sacks presented more of a puzzle. There were twenty leather bags of gold dust, each weighing five pounds, but all the bags were plain and of varying types of manufacture. The dust was pure, and it was clear that it was panned, not mined. The gold and silver coins and bills in the rest of the bags totaled over $110,000. Although most of the gains were likely ill-gotten, there was no way to trace the origin of the remainder of the money.

"If Dick Hawthorne had come over here with this pile of money, I likely would have sold him the Circle D. He didn't have to go to all that trouble, and get himself killed," quipped the colonel. The men chuckled.

"Old Dick was a busy boy," Pete said. "What's going to happen to all of this, Colonel?"

"I've been thinking about that Pete, and this is how I see it. Everyone's going to get two month's fighting wages, plus a two thousand dollar bonus. Fury and Will Morgan's next of kin get five thousand dollars. How does that sound?"

"Why, Colonel, that's more money than most of those fellows would ever see in their lifetimes—total. That's more than generous," Pete exclaimed.

"Don't try to talk him out of it, Pete," said Luke. "No one would thank you for it, including me." Everyone laughed.

"Old Dick can afford it, at least he won't care one

way or the other," the colonel said, joining the laughter. "I thought for their own good that I would pay the hands each one hundred and twenty dollars and put the two thousand dollars in a Wells Fargo account. When they see that they can make money by leaving it there, sometimes four or even six percent a year, maybe they will leave it."

"That's a great idea," Pete said. Rowdy, John, and Henry looked doubtful, but said nothing. Sing Loo nodded his head.

Luke, aware of the doubtful looks, simply said, "If we don't have it all at once, we can't spend it all at once." Everyone agreed with that.

"They took the gamble, and put themselves at risk. Nobody asked for it, but the gamble paid off. However, the men want their money, well, that's the way they can have it. I thought that they could 'see the elephant' though, with one hundred and twenty dollars in wages, that's four months normal pay. The two thousand dollars is probably more security than they ever wanted, and that's okay too," said the colonel with a sigh. "As far as that goes, anyone who was here in the fight with the Bar H can have a job at the Circle D as long as a Dawson owns it."

"I'll sure second that, Dad," Luke enthused.

"I think before spring roundup we'd better let the boys go to let off some steam. Most of them will be back, but we'd better hire a few new hands, just in case," Pete said.

"That's a good idea, Pete," the colonel said. "Let's send the boys in shifts. In the first shift, I want you to go to do some hiring. I also want to include Luke, Henry, John, Rowdy, Tex, and Sing Loo. You can include three other hands in addition to the ones I've named."

"That's a pretty top heavy group Colonel, but I guess I know why," Pete said.

"Yes, you do, Pete. In fact, I want some of the first group to join the second group going in, starting with you."

"It may be hazardous duty, but I'd like to volunteer to be in both groups," Rowdy offered. Everyone chuckled.

Chapter Twenty-three

So it was with high spirits the Circle D men rode into Dodge City that late spring of 1875. It was near noon and the sun that blazed across the sky gave off an unseasonable heat. Sing Loo drove the buckboard, having convinced the colonel of the need of more supplies, especially peaches. They passed the local stable and saw several Bar H horses for sale. The group pulled up and dismounted. Luke walked in to find the owner, a wiry man named Calico Kincaid.

"Hi there, Calico," Luke yelled.

"Why, hello Luke," Calico said. He walked out in front as he wiped his hands on his leather apron. "Haven't seen you for a few weeks, but the rumors sure been flying." The Circle D men chuckled.

"I'm sure they have." Luke laughed. "Say, we were curious about all those Bar H horses you have for sale."

"Figured you might be. Most of the sellers were headed out of town, and the only way they could get out of here was by selling their horse."

"Most of them," Pete asked.

"Yeah, there's still a Texan, name of Albaugh, recovering from gunshot wounds over at Lou's boarding house and one or two others around town. Oh, and I bought the best three of them horses from Rube Sloniker. He said no one from the Bar H would mind him selling his own horses." The Circle D men chuckled.

"Well, I guess we know who was doing the shooting with that Sharps," Henry said.

"Yep," Luke added. "And just like at the rocks, old Rube knew when to hightail it. Still and all I'm glad he didn't stick around for the fight, he probably would have bagged a few of us."

Remembering the big slugs singing by his head at the cottonwood trees, Sing Loo said, "Ah, he's no good. No good."

"Rube still around?" Luke asked.

"Nope, he bought him a wagon rig, picked up a couple skinners, and said he was going after some buffalo. Something that didn't shoot back." Calico chuckled.

The Circle D men rode on up to the General Store, where Silas Barrett was standing out front. "Why hello Luke, Sing Loo, Pete, Henry, Rowdy, Tex. It sure is good to see you boys. I haven't had much fun since you were last in town, Luke. From what I hear, you've been having all your fun out of town." The Circle D men looked at Luke and chuckled at his expense.

Luke reddened. "If that's considered fun, I could do with a little boredom."

Silas held up his smaller left arm for everyone to see his old Civil War injury. "I can sure understand that. C'mon in the store boys, it's a little cooler than out here." The men dismounted and trooped into the store. The familiar smells of the store were pleasant to them.

"Say, Luke, is what we hear right? That you took out George Sly in a standup gunfight? And after you and Sing Loo and Henry left Dodge, that you got ambushed by the Slonikers?"

"Yeah, I'm afraid so. How did you hear all this, Silas?"

"Well I heard about all four Slonikers leaving town but I heard it after you left so it was too late to warn you. Then we saw three of them come back. Rube was okay but looked pretty shook. The other two were shot up, one pretty bad, don't know if he made it or not. The other one probably recovered, but the only one I saw again was Rube. That fight with George Sly was all over Dodge City. You know how these people admire a fast gun, don't matter what you do, just as long as you're fast."

"Yeah I guess. But George Sly needed killing, he was

a murdering scum," Luke said. Even though Sly was dead, Luke was still agitated over the whole conflict, and what had caused it.

"Luke gave Sly a better chance than Sly ever gave anybody," Pete added.

"Well, with all that, and then obliterating Dick Hawthorne and the Bar H, I'd say all you boys done a good day's work and made a name for yourselves. Be careful, there might be some that just want to test you, see if you are as good as they hear."

"Confidentially Silas, that's why you see as big a group of us as there are. We don't want no trouble and we're willing to beat anybody's brains in to make sure we don't have any," Henry said. Everyone laughed. "Say, is there anything new around Dodge?"

"As a matter of fact there is. Tom LeBeau is no longer sheriff, he's dead."

"How'd that happen?" asked Henry. "I can't imagine old Tom actually tryin' to enforce the law, to the point of irritating anyone, that is." Everyone chuckled, including Silas.

"Well, it wasn't anything he was trying to enforce, it was more a commitment he wasn't keeping—like his marriage vows. It seems he took up with a local saloon gal, name of Misty Star. Don't know her real name, of course. At any rate Tom's wife, a right perky little thing named Gracie, couldn't seem to get used to the idea. That's where the trouble started."

"I'll just bet," said Pete. The others nodded in assent.

"Yep," said Silas. "When she objected to Tom's fooling around, he commenced to hitting her.

"Well, he didn't do it for long. Gracie pulled out a big Smith and Wesson and had target practice. She got him five out of six shots. After that, Tom was right peaceable—along with being dead."

"What happened to Mrs. LeBeau?" asked Rowdy.

"Yeah," said John. "With gumption like that, she sounds like a kind of gal I could admire. I even like her choice of pistols." Everyone chuckled.

"Tom LeBeau wasn't a favorite of the vigilance committee," said Silas. "I think we, I mean, they figured that he got what he deserved. Gracie will be helped to go anywhere she wants."

"So, who's the new sheriff?" asked Pete.

"Fellow named Larry Deger."

"What's he like?" asked Rowdy.

"Deger's a big fellow but not much stronger than Tom was. He's got a good deputy coming in though, fellow named Earp, Wyatt Earp."

"Heard of him," said Henry.

"Yeah, he's done some buffalo hunting and some sheriffin' up around Abilene. He's pretty fast, and uses his guns to club drunks out cold, rather than reason much with them," Silas added.

"Not a bad idea," said Luke. "We'll try to stay sober and on his good side when he gets here."

"That'd be a good idea," Silas said. Everyone nodded.

When they walked outside, who did they run into but Andrew Lewis of Wells Fargo. He still looked much more like a teamster than a businessman. He was smiling, and his brown eyes danced at the sight of Luke and the Circle D men. "Hey, there Luke, Henry, and Sing Loo, you boys have quite a crowd with you. I guess if half of what I've been hearing is true, there's a good reason for there to be this many of you."

"Andrew," Luke exclaimed. "I was hoping you were still around. I've got some things I want to discuss with you."

"That'd be great, Luke. Why don't you boys get settled, and I'll stand you all to a round at the Hoover."

After they secured rooms for the night at the Dodge House, and stabled their horses, all the Circle D men adjourned to the Hoover Saloon to have a few drinks before dinner. The Hoover was fairly typical of saloons in Dodge City. While it was of the better class, it was still a ramshackle affair. It had a long and narrow room with a bar extending about three-fourths of the way down the side wall. The odors of the saloon were familiar; dust, stale beer, whisky, and the strong smell of tobacco, both smoked and chewed. As luck would have it, when the Circle D walked in they spotted Joe Lowe with four other men at a corner table. The other men had not been at the Bar H but were obviously from Texas because they wore high boots and large rowled spurs. The left side of Joe's face was swollen, and discolored from his run in with John at the Bar H.

John Fowler looked over at Joe, and winked. Joe glowered, and said something inaudible to the rest of the table.

Andrew and Luke took a table at the other end of the bar. They were in a deep discussion and paid no attention to the Texans. Luke had just finished telling Andrew about recovering the $48,000 in Wells Fargo bags and with the wrappers still on. "It might have come from three or more robberies, Andrew, but with the letters you might be able to figure it out."

"Not me, Luke, you better take the bags directly to San Francisco and see Jerome Puddington, or even Lloyd Tevis, he's president of the whole shebang. I'm sure there will be a reward in it for you."

"It would be nice to see Jerome again. If there is any kind of a reward, we'll put it in the Circle D pot, and add it to the accounts of the hands which, by the way, we want to set up with Wells Fargo."

"All the more reason to go to San Francisco. We will be setting up an office here in Dodge City, probably can't get away from it. I wouldn't want to start off with anything of the size you're talking about, though. Besides Luke, I know you want to go to work for us and what better way is there to start out?"

"All right Andrew, but under one condition on your part."

"Name it."

"I want to open a small account with you now. If anything comes up on the Bar H land, I want you to file it in my father's name, and mine. Even if it is going up for back taxes, you will have the authority to use the account any way you see fit. We don't need another Dick Hawthorne to come in and stir things up."

"You got a deal, Luke. I'll do anything I can to help you. Especially after what you've done for Wells Fargo."

Sing Loo looked comical standing up to the bar in the Hoover Saloon, it came almost up to his shoulders. The bartender had brought out some elderberry wine from a jug stored in back, which suited Sing Loo just fine. From his last time in town he had learned not to let his queue hang down his back. This time he tucked it up under his Stetson, and dressed like the other Circle D men in custom leather boots, Levi's, and a light cotton shirt. He also carried a Colt single action pistol. Tucked in one boot he had his homemade cosh and in the other one a small knife. Sing Loo was talking, and Tex Slocum was listening, interjecting an occasional, "yup," when a loud voice interrupted from across the room. "Hey, barkeep, I didn't know you let heathens drink with decent white folk."

The bartender, Paddy O'Shea by name, was a first generation Irish immigrant. However, he had done his service in the Civil War in the Fighting Sixty-ninth out of New York. Consequently he had no use for Texans, particularly Texans of the poor, loudmouth variety. "Sure and the color of his money is just as good as yours. Better, I'm thinkin', since he pays cash, and doesn't nurse his drinks like any heathen I've ever seen, includin' the likes of you all." Paddy stretched out the all in his tenor voice as an added insult to the prideful Texans.

Pete Ryan openly smiled at Paddy's repartee, remembering how his own dad and uncles sounded around the kitchen table on a Saturday night. Luke watched as Pete caught Paddy's eye and gave him the high sign by gently shaking his head. In other words, Paddy didn't have to get involved, Sing Loo would get along just fine. Seeing Pete's signal, the big redheaded bartender busied himself at the other end of the bar, wiping it off with a rag.

With that, the Texan got up and sauntered over to the bar where Sing Loo was standing. The rest of the Circle D had turned around from the bar to watch events unfold. Had there been any apprehension on their part for Sing Loo someone like Pete or Luke would have intervened. As it was, Luke casually unthonged his Colts, since he was not sure how far this was going to go. Andrew put his thumbs in his belt, with his right hand resting just in front of his pistol, which was riding high on his hip.

Sing Loo stayed turned toward the bar, said nothing, and seemed without a care in the world. He watched in the mirror behind the bar the progress of the big Texan, who was oblivious to anyone but Sing Loo. "Joe over there tells me you boys are pretty tough, when you got the numbers on your side. Well, numbers or not, I ain't drinkin' in the same place with no heathen."

The big Texan grabbed the back of Sing Loo's right shoulder with his left hand to spin him around, his right hand was back in a cocked fist. One blow from that massive fist would kill Sing Loo. Sing Loo spun but only part way. Sing Loo's right hand was callused and hard from years of working. It was like a claw with fingers like talons of steel. His grip was as strong as a vise as the big Texan soon found out. With his back still partially to him, Sing Loo clamped on the big Texan's groin with his right hand and squeezed hard and lifted. The shocked and paralyzed Texan dropped his hand from Sing Loo's shoulder and stood up on his toes, his hands made little fluttering motions in the air as if he were trying to fly. High-pitched sounds erupted from his tortured face.

Sing Loo released his grip, turned around, and stood flatfooted, with his legs slightly bowed. Faster than even the eye could follow, he shot his fists straight from the shoulders in a blistering rapid-fire of combinations of one, then two-three. The big Texan was trying to fall down, but Sing Loo was on him so furiously that all he could do was back up.

"Hey Sing," Luke called. "Don't just use your fists, you can hurt your hand."

Pete smiled; John and Henry laughed out loud. The

rest of the Circle D was having a great time while watching the spectacle. Finally Sing Loo whirled and kicked the big Texan in the head, then he mercifully allowed the Texan to collapse on the floor unconscious.

"Ah, good," said Henry in imitation of Sing Loo, who then laughed again.

As if on signal, Pete and John walked over and picked up the big Texan, each grabbed an arm and a leg. The table where the Texans were sitting was old and scarred, but solid. Therefore, when Pete and John threw the big Texan in the middle of it, the table simply tipped over, scattering glasses, bottles, a very few coins, and the remaining Texans who were aghast at the rough treatment accorded their fellow by the little man.

"Get out," said Pete. "If you see us, avoid us. If you don't get out of our way, expect worse than what happened here. This is what you jumped-up pack of coyotes get for trying to pick on a little man."

Two of the men picked up the big Texan, while another tried to find the coins on the floor. They draped his arms around their shoulders, and walked him between them. The big Texan's head hung to one side, his eyes rolled back in his head, and his toes dragging on the floor making two crooked little trails in the dust as they all left the saloon. Joe Lowe, trailing behind his friends, tried to give a dirty look, but with the look coming from his swollen face, compliments of John Fowler, no one was much impressed.

Having completed his business with Andrew, Luke

joined in the general celebration with the Circle D. While he loved the laughter and carrying on, he didn't care for strong drink, and so limited himself to a tepid beer that he nursed throughout the festivities.

"Sure and the little man can handle himself," said Paddy. "Never have I seen anythin' quite like it."

"Paddy, you don't know the half of what Sing Loo can do," said John Fowler, who remembered the four trussed up Bar H guards and the other one, the one with the macabre smile.

"Sure and he taught some of the lads how to fight," Pete added, falling into Paddy's familiar Irish brogue. Paddy laughed, taking no offense.

Sing Loo basked in the admiration and affection of the Circle D and said, "The hand can be a weapon when you squeeze, as well as when you hit. Heh, heh."

The hands howled at that, and celebrated far into the night. As long as they were in Dodge City, they made the Hoover their primary stop, and Paddy O'Shea their friend.

Pete stayed in Dodge City along with Rowdy, Tex, and Henry to await the second group. Luke, Sing Loo, and John, along with three other Circle D hands, rode back to the ranch, with Sing Loo driving the loaded buckboard. The trip back to the Circle D was happily uneventful. As the group pulled into the yard area, the second group was saddled up and raring to go into town.

Luke gathered the group together, and outlined the

problem they'd had with the few remaining Texans and how Sing Loo had solved it. There were many appreciative chuckles. " Of course, you boys can 'see the elephant' any way you want to," said Luke. "You might want to start off with rooms at the Dodge House, then go on over to Hoover's Saloon. You'll see some of the boys there. They can give you a few tips on what else is around."

They let out some cheers but started out in only a gentle gallop. Dodge City was a long way off, and they didn't want to wind their horses.

Luke went inside, and sat down with the colonel. Over the last few days the colonel's vigor was slowly returning, but it seemed a slow process to Luke who was used to seeing his dad healthy, and in charge. Luke briefed the colonel fully on his meeting with Andrew Lewis.

"What do you want to do, son," asked the colonel.

"Well, I definitely want to help with the roundup. When the boys all get back together we're going to have our work cut out for us between the Circle D and Bar H stock. One thing I was curious and meant to ask Pete about though."

"What's that, Luke?"

"I saw some of our cattle out north, and it looked like their Circle D brands were fading. How could that be?"

The colonel shook his head, and could only smile. "That Dick Hawthorne, if Rowdy hadn't done such a good job on him I would have hanged him for sure."

"Why, Dad? I mean, what else did he do?"

"The cattle you saw were wet branded."

"What's that?"

"Wet branding is when you put a wet towel between the branding iron and the cattle. It singes the hair but not the skin so the brand grows out, after a short time, leaving an unbranded cow."

"Leaving an unbranded cow that can be rounded up at a later time and another brand put on it—like the Bar H," Luke asked.

"That's what he would have done, Luke. I'm glad you noticed, now we're going to have to re-brand a lot of our own cattle."

So it was that when the Circle D all assembled to go back to work, that they had to check their own cattle to make sure that the brands were good. Throughout the spring and summer all the hands along with a few new ones that Pete had hired worked hard to round up all the Circle D and Bar H animals. While the Bar H-branded animals were not strictly owned by the Circle D, the colonel figured possession was all that mattered. If it came to that, he could call the animals "mavericks" and make it stick.

The colonel spoke with Luke about his coming trip to San Francisco, to Wells Fargo headquarters. "People get killed for four dollars, let alone forty-eight thousand dollars."

"I know, Dad," Luke said. "That's why I'd like to

take Sing and Henry with me. I've seen them both in action, and I won't have any worries about my back being covered. Besides, I'd like to see what Wells Fargo is going to offer."

"All right, Luke," the colonel replied. "Now that spring roundup is done, you might as well go on and get this business with Wells Fargo taken care of. I reckon Pete and I can handle the Circle D for a while."

Luke laughed. "I'm glad to see you're getting your sense of humor back, Dad. You and Pete can handle the Circle D for another thirty years."

The colonel chuckled. "Maybe not that long, but we'll be okay. You just watch out for danger, from any and all sides."

"Don't worry Dad, after what we went through with the Bar H, the trip to San Francisco should be like a walk along the river."

Henry and Sing Loo were excited about the trip to San Francisco. While Sing Loo had helped to build and maintain the railroad, he had rarely ridden on one. Henry and Luke had only seen the trains, and had never ridden them. Luke split up the money into six packages to go in the saddlebags. Their armament was similar to that which they carried before the big fight with the Bar H, with Sing Loo still preferring the shotgun and Luke and Henry carrying Winchesters. In addition to their sidearms, Colt revolvers, each man carried a small hideout pistol either tucked in the top of a boot or in the back of a belt. Also, they loaded up an extra packhorse with food, ammunition, and blankets for the relatively short ride up to North Platte, in Nebraska. Luke wanted to get to the uninhabited western part of the Union Pacific line beyond Fort Kearney. He thought, rightfully so, that the fewer people that saw them carrying the saddlebags the better.

Chapter Twenty-four

They started out at dawn that summer day, and the coming heat of the day was foretold by the brightness of the sun. Since it was summertime, the rivers were low and therefore presented no problems when it came time to cross. The boys merely tied their boots around their necks and swam the horses across. That night, with Sing Loo along, the boys ate royally, having fried steak, potatoes, biscuits, and molasses topped off with as many cups of Arbuckle's coffee as they could drink.

Next morning they were up at the crack of dawn again. Mid-morning they came to the Republican River, where an enterprising fellow had built a toll ferry complete with a rope as a guide, to pull across passen-

186

gers. The ferryman sized up his customers, and judged their ability to pay. "It'll be one dollar a horse to arrive dry on the other side," he said.

"I heard you had a bad crop last year," said Luke. "I didn't think you would try to get it all back with one ferry trip."

"Matter of fact, we did have a bad year," the man said sourly. "The grasshoppers ate more than we did. That's the price, take it or leave it."

"Tell you what," said Henry. "We'll shoot you for it, double or nothing."

"I ain't that good a shot," said the man.

"No, that ain't what I mean," said Henry. "All we have to do is miss, and we pay you double. Luke here will throw up a silver cartwheel, and I'll hit it. Then I'll throw up two half dollars at the same time, and Luke will hit them. Then we owe you nothing."

"And you'll use six-guns, not the shotgun that there little feller is carrying?"

"We'll use the six-guns," said Luke with a big smile.

"This I got to see," said the ferryman. "Let's open the ball."

Henry and Luke dismounted, as did Sing Loo, and they all stretched. Luke took out a silver dollar and flipped it high in the air. Henry drew and fired in one smooth motion. He hit the dollar with his first shot, knocking it higher. Henry waited a fraction of a second for it to drop, and fired again hitting it a second time.

"Huh," said the ferryman. "That there is some good shootin'. You didn't even have to hit it that second time."

"Aw, I just had to show old Luke there that I could shoot a little," said Henry. "Last time I tried that it didn't come out so hot."

Luke laughed, and relaxed, his hands at his waist. Henry flipped two half dollars into the air. Using his lightning draw, Luke's pistols leaped into his hands. He fired with each pistol before either coin reached its apex, they each rose higher after being struck. Luke then fired twice again, after only a slight hesitation, and hit each half-dollar again, sending them off ringing about twenty yards away.

"Boys, that there is the best pistol shootin' I ever seen," exclaimed the ferryman. "If I hadn't seen it with my own eyes, I'd never have believed it. You boys sure earned free passage."

"Tell you what," Luke offered. "Why don't you find the coins we shot, and keep them for the fare? Two dollars is just about what you would usually charge us anyway, isn't it?"

"Yeah," the ferryman answered sheepishly. "You're right. Say, no offense boys. I'm just tryin' to make a livin,' and you boys looked more prosperous than most."

"None taken," Henry said with a laugh. "It was good to get in a little target practice."

The ferryman's observation of their prosperous look made the boys more cautious in their travel. By agreement, they didn't bunch together, and when they came to the occasional rolling hill they spread out, watching even more carefully. The rest of the trip was uneventful, however, and when the boys rode across the Clarke Bridge on the Platte River, they were fairly relaxed.

They only had to wait four hours for the big Union Pacific wood-burner to come huffing and puffing into the small stop, at North Platte. A dragon could not have conjured up more cinder, smoke, and sparks to come out of the huge smokestack. After they secured their horses in an animal car, the boys found seats up front. The hard-backed wooden benches were not as comfortable as a saddle, but the train went at a steady pace, twenty miles per hour, day and night with few stops.

At the start of their trip, one of the eastern passengers brought a new Winchester out of his luggage, and began shooting from the train out the window. No one was much bothered until they came upon a small herd of buffalo, and the man downed a couple of them. The shooter was a big man with a florid face which framed a small mustache. He wore a black suit, and a derby hat. He was proudly reloading his rifle and looked up curiously when Henry walked over to him. "Don't do that," Henry ordered, by way of introduction.

The man looked at Henry and frowned. "And who are you to tell me not to shoot, and why should I stop?"

"I'll take the second part of your question first," Henry said. "Because it's a waste. I've hunted these buffalo, and it pains me some to see an idiot like you killin' them for no good reason."

Looking at Henry through narrowed eyes the man said, "And the first part?"

Henry smiled, his eyes crinkled. "Who am I to tell you not to shoot?"

"That's right," the man said.

"That's easy, I'll tell you who I am. I'm the fellow who's going to throw you off this train, and let you survive by eating what you've killed. 'Course there might be some Indians around who might not take kindly to you. But that shouldn't bother you, brave fellow like you. I'll just bet they'll be real impressed with that fancy suit."

The man's expression changed from one of indignation to one of shock. "But—but you couldn't just throw me off the train."

Still smiling, Henry said, "Mister, who's going to know? Out here the only thing a man has, sometimes, is his word. I give you my word, you kill another buffalo, or any other living thing, and you're going off the train, and it won't be at a scheduled stop."

The man took in Henry's garb, and his armament. He looked back to where Henry had been sitting, at Luke and Sing Loo. They both stared impassively back. The man brought in his Winchester from the window, and began jacking the shells out of the magazine. A few of the shells made sharp little sounds, heard above the clatter of the train, as they hit the hardwood floor and rolled. Henry walked back to his seat, still smiling.

Luke and Sing Loo chuckled. The easterner glowered, but then only stared out the window, and gazed long-ingly at the buffalo herd.

A little while later, one of the easterner's fellow pas-sengers came up to him. "Hey there, Cliff, if you're not going to do any shootin', how about lettin' me? I want to bag me a buffalo."

"I wouldn't do that," the easterner said in a low voice.

"How come?"

"Some folks around here get downright hostile when you do."

"Oh, pshaw, lemme have that gun. No one's going to tell me what to do."

"You were warned," said Cliff. He got up and, after a furtive glance back at Henry, rushed out of the car.

"Sure, sure, I was warned," said the second man to the easterner's back. Then he aimed the Winchester out the window—

About fifteen minutes later, having heard no firing, Cliff, the easterner, came back. On the wooden bench lay his Winchester. His fellow passenger was nowhere to be seen. The easterner put away his rifle in the case and sat down. He glanced back at the boys, who were all staring innocently out the window. He didn't say anything for the rest of the trip.

The views of the mountains were beautiful and, of the Nevada and California desert, picturesque. Sparks and smoke would sometimes come in through the window, particularly when making a sweeping turn or, if the wind was wrong. Luke marveled at the great expanse of the country.

There were always two of the three boys guarding the bags, while not pretending to do so. While the conductor stared balefully at the men's heavy armament, particularly Sing Loo's, he understood the westerners' need for self-protection however, and said nothing.

A few days later they arrived in San Francisco in mid-morning. Luke and Henry were awed with the size and the hustle and bustle of the city. "I've never seen anything like this in all my born days," exclaimed Henry.

"Me neither," Luke added. "Just a few pictures and they don't begin to tell the story."

Sing Loo, like most of his countrymen, had entered the country at San Francisco, and therefore remembered what it was like. "Ah, there's good food here. I won't have to cook. Heh, heh." The other two smiled.

The boys put their horses in a livery stable, and hired a cart to take them to the Wells Fargo offices. Luke had sent a telegram to Jerome Puddington from North Platte, and while it was received in San Francisco, he had no way of knowing if it had been actually delivered.

They were a tired looking trio when they walked into the big three-story building on California and Montgomery Street. Also, they were dusty and unshaven from being on the train. A big man, pompous in a blue uniform with brass buttons, came bustling up. "You gentlemen have business with Wells Fargo?"

Luke straightened up and looked him in the eye. "We're here to see Jerome Puddington or Lloyd Tevis."

"And what, may I ask, is the nature of your business?"

"Now that you mention it, you may not ask," Luke deadpanned, not liking the man's attitude at all. "Just tell them Luke Dawson and two friends are here."

"You wait here." The man turned on his heel and left.

Within three minutes Jerome came bounding down the stairs, followed closely by a man with a slightly receding hairline, his hair worn long, over the ears, and a full beard, shot through with gray, and no mustache; Lloyd Tevis. His blue eyes were lively and piercing. He had a high, wide forehead, giving one the impression of deep intellect. The astonished big man in the blue uniform was finishing a distant third. Luke noticed the surprised expression on Jerome's face as he looked back at Tevis. Apparently Lloyd Tevis rarely came out to greet anyone. He wore a black suit and a bright white shirt with a short wing collar. Around the collar was a small exposed bow tie.

"Luke, Henry, Sing Loo, it's great to see all of you." Jerome then conducted the introductions. Everyone shook hands all around.

"I understand if anyone's hunting trouble, it's not a good idea to pick on you three," Lloyd said with a rapid-fire bark. The trio smiled.

"Well, let's go up to my office. Bring the bags. Here, let me help. Ed, watch this baggage, and stick around, I may want you to drive them somewhere. No, wait, I want you to go to the Palace Hotel and secure three of their best rooms for the week on Wells Fargo. If you have any trouble, ask for Mr. Ralston and tell him it's for me. You can put their baggage back in a storage room for now." Lloyd Tevis' voice was quick, and intense, as was the man.

"Yes, sir, Mr. Tevis, sir," Ed, the man in blue, said. With that he was moving in a blur.

The boys, and Jerome, trooped into Lloyd Tevis's office. Luke saw by a plaque that Tevis had been president of Wells Fargo since 1872. He knew from Jerome that all the direction of the company originated with him. His office was large and festooned with mahogany, brass, and leather as befitted the president of a large, growing, company.

Tevis looked at the three men. "Jerome tells me that you have had quite a few adventures. He told me firsthand about Dodge City and those buffalo hunters. However, about the actual recovery of this money, he was a little sketchy, having heard it from Andrew who heard it from you, Luke. Do you mind if I hear it firsthand?"

Luke began the story starting with the attempt on his father's life and the range war. Henry interrupted, "Lloyd, I know you want to hear the story, but if I let Luke here tell it, it's going to be as dry as last year's hay." Everybody chuckled, including Luke. "You might say I was a very interested observer." Henry fingered the holes in his Stetson as he began the story. He looked at Jerome. "You remember the Slonikers."

Jerome nodded his head. "Very well."

"Well, sir, after we left Dodge City..." Henry told about the ambush by the Slonikers and Luke's solution with his high angle shooting. He continued about the Bar H, and the confrontation with George Sly, and the final battle with the Bar H, and the discovery of the Wells Fargo money. He was very colorful in telling his story, evoking gasps at the high points from his two interested listeners.

"And it was all Luke's plan," Henry said in conclusion. "Right out of the Book of Joshua, eighth chapter."

Tevis nodded his head, deep in thought. He looked at Jerome. "You ever hear of this George Sly?"

Jerome nodded his head. "Just like Henry described him, a real snake."

"It sounds like the world is well rid of the bunch of them. I wonder, could this Dick Hawthorne have been Dick Hayward, a fellow who robbed us with a gang, plenty, earlier on?"

Jerome sat up. "I hadn't thought about it, but you are probably right. He gave us a lot of grief in our early days. You men did outstanding work."

Luke interjected, "Thanks, it's true, the plan was mine but Henry and Sing Loo each accounted, personally, for a lot more of the Bar H men than I did."

"There's more than enough credit to go around. Now, to business." Tevis was brisk. He and Jerome looked over the contents of the saddlebags.

"I suppose a sharp lawyer could explain the money in

the Wells Fargo wrappers, but not the letters too," Tevis observed. "Dick Hawthorne or Hayward must have been supremely arrogant to have kept them all together."

"He wasn't what you'd call a shy man," said Luke. The ghost of a smile crossed Tevis' countenance.

"Here's what Wells Fargo will do," said Tevis, again, all business. "Twenty-five percent of the recovered monies, that's twelve thousand, will go to the Circle D. In addition, I will include a two thousand dollar reward for Dick Hawthorne as the leader of the gang. It's probably not enough, but much more than the five hundred we usually pay. The Palace is the best hotel in San Francisco. You three have a week there, all expenses paid including meals, which are sumptuous. Additionally, there will be two hundred dollars allocated to each of you for incidental expenses. You may also have railroad passes to take you anywhere you want.

"Finally, I want to express the deep, deep appreciation of Wells Fargo, and myself, for your courage and efforts. If there's ever anything we can do in the way of a favor, you need only ask. I understand even before all this that Jerome was in discussion with you, Luke, and you, Henry, about possible employment with Wells Fargo." They both nodded their heads in assent.

Tevis continued. "I would also like to extend an offer to you, Sing Loo. I believe we can find a place for you in our organization."

Sing Loo nodded once in acknowledgement, then slowly shook his head. "I thank you, sir, for your kind offer. The hotel, I accept most gratefully. The job I think—no, I have seen much of life and have no need to see more excitement. The Circle D is my home, and will be until I die."

Luke looked at the little man who had taught him so much, and felt a lot of affection for him. There was moisture in his eyes. Sing Loo considered the Circle D home, his permanent home, just as much as Luke himself did. Now they were about to go on divergent paths, it would be strange without Sing.

"I fully appreciate what you said, Sing Loo. It is indeed a rare man who knows where he wants to be forever. Thanks, anyway. Jerome, I think you should take the men to your office and discuss the possibilities of their further involvement with Wells Fargo."

After again shaking hands all around, they repaired to Jerome's office. "Nothing much has changed since I last talked to you in Dodge City except that now, we can really use you both," Jerome said, by way of opening the conversation.

"That's great," Luke answered. "Isn't it, Henry?"

"Sure is," Henry agreed. "Sounds like it might be a bit different from ranch work, though."

"It is different," Jerome said, as he looked searchingly at the two men. "However, in the light of your recent experiences with the Bar H, I can't say that it's any more dangerous." Luke and Henry smiled.

"There is one thing, though, when you're an undercover agent for Wells Fargo, you're on your own. You won't know for sure what person you can trust or even if you have any friends at all." This time, Henry and Luke nodded without any trace of a smile.

Jerome continued, "You have to assess every local situation. You have to determine if the law is honest, corrupt, or maybe, just plain weak. Also, you may not want to identify yourself to the local Wells Fargo agent and choose instead to remain totally undercover. You will have to look at these, and many other factors, to best determine how you are going to do your job as an agent of Wells Fargo."

Long into the afternoon they discussed the duties, responsibilities, and ramifications of being a Wells Fargo undercover agent. "By definition," Jerome pointed out, "undercover means that you have to have another occupation. This means working in something around, or related to, the commerce of the local area. You won't find out much as a ranch hand, but it might be necessary to pose as one, from time to time, particularly when you travel. You might even have to pose as a gambler, but try not to lose too much, Wells Fargo can't afford to subsidize bad habits." All of them chuckled. "The main thing is, you may be reassigned on a moment's notice, so you have to be ready to move, quickly. For the most part however, your assignments will be such that you will have time to work in to the local area, and thereby uncover what is necessary for your job."

"It sounds to me," Luke observed, "that this job takes a lot of good common sense." Henry nodded.

"That's about eighty percent of it," agreed Jerome.

"What's the rest of it?" Henry inquired.

"Nerve, skill with firearms, and a determination to see the job through."

"I reckon we both qualify on all counts," Luke observed. "We're both probably too stubborn to stop before a job is through."

Henry laughed. "Even if a body needs a powerful lot of persuading that we're just doin' our job, they'll get the message, one way or the other."

Luke smiled and slowly nodded his head. Jerome smiled and stood up. "Welcome to Wells Fargo, both of you. Your pay is one hundred and fifty dollars per month deposited wherever you want. Also, all of your expenses are covered." Jerome was well aware that all three men already had sizeable accounts in Wells Fargo. Still, $150 a month was more than double what a top cowhand anywhere would make. *They will be well worth all that, and then some.*

The Palace Hotel was the lap of luxury in old San Francisco. The rooms were large and luxurious. The carpets were thick, the beds were high four-posters, and the overstuffed furniture was upholstered in velvet. The food, as advertised, was varied and the best anywhere. The boys toured the town and had a great time. They stayed away from the Barbary Coast, however, on the advice of Jerome. Why look for trouble? They felt that they'd had more than their fair share of trouble in a short amount of time. All the same, they had fun. It seemed that the name Tevis, coupled with Wells Fargo, could unlock any door they wanted.

After a day, Sing Loo disappeared. He came back two days later with a big smile on his face. When Luke ventured to ask him where he had been, Sing Loo only smiled and said, "I had business, but I took care of it. Heh heh."

On the night that Sing Loo was gone, Jerome came over to the hotel and had dinner with Luke and Henry. "How do you like the food here, boys?"

"Don't tell Sing Loo, I wouldn't want to hurt his feelings, but it's the best I've ever had," Luke answered.

Henry nodded. "Say, what do you call this white meat again?"

"That's lobster, Henry," answered Jerome.

"Sure is good."

"Yep, sure is," Luke agreed.

"Say, would you boys like to see a high stakes poker game in the back? Maybe sit in a few hands?"

"I don't know about sitting in, but it might be fun to watch a few hands," Luke said. "What do you think, Henry?"

"Sounds okay to me."

"All right," Jerome said. "Let's go, I'll introduce you around."

Toward the back, there was a table in play, four men fully engrossed in their game. The tables were round and covered in green velvet tablecloths. Overhead, the cut glass chandeliers were partly obscured by tendrils of smoke circling round and about. No one looked up as Jerome, Luke, and Henry entered. Jerome made quiet introductions of Luke and Henry as being from "back east," while the players merely glanced up and nodded their heads. The smell of cigar smoke was pervasive. A table off to the side had an array of bottles and glasses and a large bucket of ice. Standing at the table, at semi-attention, was a bellman.

The players all looked as if they had used the same tailor. Their suits were of a fashionable cut and were uniformly black. Two of the men had cravats with large diamond stickpins, the rest had bow ties of varying styles. All of the men had big thick gold watch chains across their fronts. In contrast, Luke and Henry were dressed in their casual western-style clothes and had only recently acquired jackets to wear over them, primarily to conceal their weapons. The open carrying of firearms was frowned upon in "civilized" San Francisco.

Jerome, Luke, and Henry sat off to the side and watched the play for a while. While Luke had not had a lot of experience actually gambling, he did have a great deal of experience in spotting cheaters. The colonel and Wild Bill had schooled Luke thoroughly in spotting all kinds of cheating devices. It was, therefore, with some amusement that he noticed that two of the "gentlemen" gamblers were cheating, at the same table. Eric Holcomb, also known as Blue Chip was a regular around San Francisco. He stood six feet tall with a medium build, brown receding hairline and darting blue eyes that accentuated his nervous mannerisms. The fact that he seemed to study the backs of other cards as much as he studied the front of his own seemed just a part of his eccentricities. Luke, with his keen eyesight, didn't need to study the backs of the cards, he could tell that they were marked, very cleverly, and intricately, but still marked.

The other fellow, sitting across, was known as "Diamond Jim Walsh." Diamond Jim had diamond cuff links, stickpin, and on his left pinkie, a large diamond ring. The ring was also known as a "shiner," in less savory circles, so that whenever Jim dealt the cards, he could see what they were, simply by turning the diamond in toward him. Luke couldn't tell if the two were in cahoots or not. If they were, they certainly seemed to be working at cross-purposes, although both men were winning the big pots with great regularity.

After watching for a while Luke beckoned Jerome and Henry out into the hall. He looked at Jerome. "I don't know how to tell you this but Blue Chip and Diamond Jim are both cheating."

Henry had a wry grin. "I guess it doesn't matter what kind of duds you put on, if a body's a cheat, he'll be a cheat no matter what."

Jerome's mouth dropped open. "Luke are you sure? I mean those two have been fixtures here at the Palace for months now. They don't always play together, either. How could they?" Luke briefly explained the methods of both men.

"Well I'll be. Luke do you think you could beat them—at their own game?"

Luke scratched his head, thinking. "It's not easy, Jerome. Blue Chip knows every card in the deck and Diamond Jim knows every card that he himself deals."

Jerome crinkled his forehead. "I've got an idea about that diamond, I think we can take care of it."

Luke thought a bit longer. "Here's what you do—"

A few minutes later, the bellman came out of the room to get some more liquor. Jerome spoke to him, money changed hands, the bellman went on his way. Jerome, Luke, and Henry all walked back into the room and resumed their places from before. The other two gamblers had decided to call it a night. Blue Chip offered Jerome a vacant chair. Jerome nodded and looked over at Luke. "Do you want the other one?"

Luke got up. "Sure, I'll sit in a couple of hands. The stakes look high though."

"Tell you what," Diamond Jim expansively declared, "we'll make it twenty to open and raises at no more than fifty. That shouldn't break anybody, should it?"

"Maybe not the first hand anyway," Luke said. "I wouldn't want to hold you gentlemen back from your regular game though."

"Don't worry about that," Blue Chip interjected. "We'll just keep it a friendly game."

Luke looked back and forth. "Sounds good to me."

The game progressed in a desultory fashion with no one winning or losing very much. Luke ordered a prearranged butter and rum drink, very heavy on the butter. When it arrived, he placed the drink on his right and Diamond Jim Walsh's left. Luke took a very small sip, set the drink down and waited. When it came to Diamond Jim's deal he reached out for the cards and Luke reached out to help. Inadvertently, so it seemed, Luke knocked over his drink, and it spilled onto Diamond Jim's left hand and the cards. It created one big, greasy mess, and both Blue Chip and Diamond Jim swore softly.

"I'm right sorry about that," Luke exclaimed. "I got it on your pretty ring and ruined the cards and everything." Henry looked up at the ceiling to keep from smiling.

Jerome looked over at the bellman. "Son, would you get us a new deck of cards?"

"Right away, sir," the bellman replied and left. He returned a few minutes later with a sealed deck of cards.

Diamond Jim had wiped off his hands and the game began in earnest. The new deck of cards had a plain design on the back and nothing on the corners. Blue Chip scowled at the design on the cards. Diamond Jim kept looking at his pinkie ring and rubbing his finger. It was obvious that the stone was now clouded with grease, and it would take a good long soaking, in hot water and soap, to get the stone clear again.

"Something wrong?" Luke asked, all wide-eyed and innocent.

"Nothing, nothing at all," growled Diamond Jim. "Let's play poker."

And they did play, but without the advantage of knowing what the other fellow's cards were, Blue Chip and Diamond Jim played very badly. After about an hour, with both down about $1,000, they began to stretch and give out exaggerated yawns. "Well, I'm about ready to call it a night," Diamond Jim said.

"Yep, me too," added Blue Chip.

"Okay," Luke drawled. "There is just one thing, though."

"Yeah?" Diamond Jim snarled, a hint of suspicion in his voice. "What's that?"

Luke reached behind him and grabbed a Bowie knife attached to his holster rig. He brought the knife out and stabbed it into the table top about half an inch from Diamond Jim's left hand. Diamond Jim recoiled in surprise and fear.

"This," Luke spat out, "in some towns back east, if they caught you using a shiner like that big diamond, they might cut off your finger for a souvenir."

"Well, I never," Blue Chip said.

"Don't you act all surprised, Blue Chip," Luke continued. "I figured if he could read the backs of the cards, the way you can, old Diamond Jim here wouldn't have had to try so hard to see what he was dealing. I'll show you what I mean."

With that Luke gathered the remnants of the first deck of cards, put them face down and proceeded to read off every one correctly and then flipped them over. "I don't know if you two are the dumbest or just the clumsiest cheats I've ever seen. Two thousand dollars is cheap compared to what it could cost you."

"Boys," Jerome interjected, looking at Diamond Jim and Blue Chip. "I can imagine what you might be thinking right now but I've seen Luke and Henry shoot. If you have any thoughts that way, make them short because that's how long your lives will be—short. Now, I know you're both heeled, so put your weapons up on the table."

Henry stood up, very alert, his hands held loosely at his sides. Luke scooted back from the table, and unthonged his Colts. The bellman went over to a far table and ducked down. With sighs, both men put an assortment of Sharps derringers and Remington derringers on the table.

"I understand why you cheat," Jerome continued. "You're both lousy poker players when you have to play straight. As of now you are both banned from the Palace Hotel. When word of this game gets out, and it will, you might find it healthier somewhere, anywhere, else. In other words, you've got about twelve hours to get out of San Francisco"

Without another word, or a backward look, both cheaters got up and left.

"I thought I'd seen everything." Jerome laughed. "Two cheaters, working independently at the same table."

"Where'd you hear that about grease and diamonds, Jerome?" asked Henry.

"Yeah, Jerome," said Luke. "I thought I was going to gag on that drink I had to take a sip of."

Jerome chuckled. "If I'd been sitting in your spot, I'd have had to take that small sip instead of you and then aim it at Diamond Jim's pinkie and the cards. But to answer your question, it's one of the ways they use to separate diamonds from everything else, by using grease. It clouds them up so they can be identified, then they have to be soaked in hot water and soap for quite awhile. A friend of mine named Kevin Mulroy taught me that trick."

"It's a good one," Luke observed. "Here, let's divide these poker winnings."

"Yeah, three ways," Jerome added.

"Aw," Henry said. "I didn't do nothin' except watch."

"Except when it came to facing down those cheats Henry, you were right there," Jerome said as he looked at Henry.

Henry looked back at Jerome and Luke. "Well, okay, gosh, thanks."

Luke counted out his share. "We've got some pretty good accounts in Wells Fargo."

Jerome nodded his head. "We're paying four percent in January and in June now."

Henry did a moment's calculation. "Why, gosh, I'm making almost now in interest what I did as a cowhand on the Circle D."

Luke laughed. "Just imagine how much the big boys

are making off our money. I'll leave mine in there though."

"Me, too," Henry agreed.

The boys had a good time for the rest of their stay in the city. They had all the fresh seafood they could eat and spent a lot of time down at the wharf watching the ships come and go and all the seafront activities.

The day before they were to leave they went back to the Wells Fargo offices one more time for their assignments. They were going to meet with Jerome in his office when Lloyd Tevis came bounding in.

"I just wanted to say again welcome to Wells Fargo, Henry and Luke. Jerome told me about the other night at the Palace. That's the way to go, put a hot ramrod to those cheats. Well, anyway, I just wanted to say I'm looking forward to hearing about you. If ever you need anything and Jerome's not around, just call on me."

Luke and Henry expressed their thanks and with that Lloyd went back to his own office. Jerome got down to the business of making their assignments. "After you boys go back and get your things in order at the Circle D, here's where I want you to go. Henry, I want you to start with our operations in the Northwest Territory. Luke, you'll work your way up to the Dakotas and work around our operations there."

The boys had just checked out of the Palace Hotel and were heading back to the railroad station. A shot rang out closely followed by a second one. Luke felt a tug as his hat flew off his head. Henry and Sing Loo dropped their luggage and dived into the street.

Luke crouched and drew both of his Colts from under his jacket. He saw a blur to his left and looked. There was Diamond Jim drawing another bead on Luke with a Colt single action pistol. Luke fired once, twice. Diamond Jim did a half turn and fell. The explosions in the confined area rang loud and frightening. This wasn't Dodge City, this was San Francisco, and there was pandemonium. Horses were pawing the air in front of their carriages. Men and women were screaming and diving for cover.

Henry drew a pistol and looked off to the right. There was Blue Chip with a pistol in his hand sprinting away trying for the corner of a building. Henry fired and dropped him. The screams got louder.

After everything calmed down it took Jerome talking to the local constabulary to get the three boys out of difficulty. The city took a dim view of gunfights no matter the reason.

"I guess those two just didn't want to quietly leave the city," said Henry.

"They will now," Luke dryly observed.

It was a subdued trio that rode the train back to North Platte. The brass oval passes that the boys now displayed made the conductor think that they were seasoned travelers. The days were getting hotter but the breeze coming in from the passenger car windows helped cool them off. Luke realized for the first time that when he got himself in trouble, Henry and Sing Loo would not be there to guard his back. Henry was entertaining similar thoughts. He had greatly enjoyed some of the high jinks he and Luke had gotten into. He would have to be much more careful now. Along with Luke, he had taken Jerome's instructions to heart.

Sing Loo's thoughts were also of a melancholy nature. He would miss Luke, who had saved his life in a confrontation that now seemed so long ago. From that chance meeting, and his association with the Circle D, Sing Loo had acquired a great deal of wealth. This wealth would be considered even greater among his countrymen. He had invested only half of his money with Wells Fargo. The other half he had taken to Chinatown and invested in some low-risk, high-yield ventures. Sing Loo had been swiftly and respectfully invited to join these ventures after he had permanently settled some accounts with two very bad men. They had been a main part of a ring that had put Sing Loo and countless others into virtual slavery upon their arrival from China. It turned out the bad men weren't nearly as bad as they thought they were. They disappeared without any serious inquiry being made. While Sing Loo could have settled into a comfortable retirement in San Francisco, he simply wasn't ready. It was as he said to Lloyd Tevis, he loved his life on the Circle D. Besides, now that Luke was going, he felt the colonel would need him more than ever.

After getting off the train at North Platte, the boys rode back down to the Republican River. The ferryman was a changed man and greeted them like long lost kinfolk. "Say there boys, glad to see you again. Now why didn't you tell me who you were, and that you all were with the Circle D?"

"Didn't think it would make a difference," Luke answered.

"Make a difference! Well, I swan, you all are famous."

"Famous?" Henry asked.

"As if you didn't know," the ferryman continued. "I could have sold these here coins you all plugged a hundred times over. That fight with the Bar H is known all over the territory. Never did meet him of course, but I hear that Sly was fast, real fast. And that there showdown with George Sly is getting to be a legend. Now I hear about some fracas in 'Frisco."

"I guess there's no help for that," Luke said softly and regretfully.

"Nope, but I'll tell you what, this trip across the river is on me."

"Naw," said Henry, "we can't let you do that but thanks for the offer. Tell you what, we'll shoot some more coins for you and you can sell them. Okay, Luke?"

"Sure, why not? The tenth chapter of Luke tells us, 'The laborer is worthy of his hire,' just so he doesn't try to get his 'worthy' all at once, like off of us."

They all chuckled and the ferryman was quite happy to walk away with four half dollars plugged by Luke and Henry. These coins he would sell for a lot more than their face value.

Riding back into the Circle D, Sing Loo came out with a characteristic, "Ah, good." It was good to be home. His home.

Luke and Henry sat down with the colonel and Pete. They had a long frank discussion about Wells Fargo and the opportunities accorded them by such a move. The colonel had realized that it was time for Luke to see the world for himself. He shook his head about the story of the card cheaters and the bloody aftermath and said, "What you saw there was only a mild dose of what it will be like in the more wide open towns. You boys be careful and keep your backs to the wall. Remember from the Book of Proverbs, Chapter Twenty-seven, 'He that meddles in strife not his own, is like taking a dog by the ears.' In other words mind your own business, don't go getting chewed on by something you don't need to. You both will have a lot of adventure just doing your own jobs, don't go looking for trouble."

Luke and Henry both promised to take time off and come back for roundups at the Circle D. The ranch was now a home to Henry, and Luke knew that Henry would also greatly miss the colonel and the Circle D.

Just before they were ready to head out, John Fowler walked up to Luke and held out a big hand. Luke greeted John warmly, and they looked each other in the eye. "Luke, the best luck I ever had was when I lost that fight to you. Now, I have a great job, the best grub, and more money than I ever saw in one place. All thanks to me bein' full of myself and thinkin' I could lick the world."

"John, the best luck I had was when I never had to fight you again. You forget, I've seen you in action, and—no thanks."

"Well, the best of luck to you, Luke. If you ever need something, anything, all you got to do is holler. I'll be there faster than you can say scat."

Luke smiled at this big tough man who had become his friend. "Thanks John, I really do appreciate that. I hope I don't have to holler, but if I do, I will, and you'll be the one I'll holler for." John smiled back, the crinkling of his eyes accented his scarred face and bent nose.

Sing Loo walked up. "Good-bye, Luke. I will be here but I will miss you."

"Good-bye, Sing. I'll be back for roundup, so you won't even know I've been gone."

"I will know, Luke."

It was the start of another gorgeous day that would soon turn hot. Luke and Henry started out together but soon parted up at North Platte. Luke felt a slight stinging sensation in his eyes at his final parting from Henry, he thought it probably was caused by the dust.

Luke was looking forward to his employment with

Wells Fargo. He knew he would miss his dad and all the men at the ranch. Still, what better way to see the country and meet new people and have some adventure. If he only knew the half of it.